She hesitated, hardly daring to breathe…

Janine recognized him instantly the moment he turned around. It was the man she'd fallen in love with, but who had vanished one night without even saying goodbye. She'd given up all hope of finding him....

"How do you do," he said, politely extending his hand. Why was he treating her like a stranger?

As their hands touched, she felt the cold metal of his wedding ring…and the icy stare of the woman suddenly beside him.

Other

MYSTIQUE BOOKS

by CLAUDETTE VIRMONNE

For a free catalogue listing all available Mystique Books,
send your name and address to:

MYSTIQUE BOOKS
M.P.O. Box 707, Niagara Falls, NY 14302
In Canada: 649 Ontario St., Stratford, Ontario N5A 6W2

Dark Side of Love

by CLAUDETTE VIRMONNE

MYSTIQUE BOOKS

TORONTO · LONDON · NEW YORK
HAMBURG · AMSTERDAM · STOCKHOLM

DARK SIDE OF LOVE/first published March 1981

Copyright © 1981 by Worldwide Library.
Copyright © MCMLXXVIII by Librairie Jules Tallandier, as
CET AMOUR D'UN SOIR
Philippine copyright 1981. Australian copyright 1981.

ISBN 0-373-50120-X

PRINTED IN CANADA

PROLOGUE

The two men at the corner table drew many looks of admiration and curiosity from the women strolling by on the Champs-Elysées, but they were deep in conversation and didn't seem to notice.

The elder of the two—a startlingly handsome dark-haired man with intense green eyes and a deep cleft in his chin—signaled a passing waiter and ordered more wine, then turned back to his companion.

"I don't know how to tell you this, except to be very direct," said the younger man, his face very serious now. "It's all very awkward. She's...pregnant." His voice had dropped to a barely audible whisper.

"*Pregnant?*" the dark-haired man exploded, then darted his eyes around nervously, realizing that he'd almost shouted the word.

Collecting himself, and making sure to lower his voice so that no one else at the sidewalk café would overhear, he went on, "But that's hardly likely! It's not...well, I suppose *anything's* possible with her. Are you sure?"

The younger man nodded morosely, his curly blond hair shimmering in the afternoon sun. "She told me this morning."

"This will kill the count," the dark-haired man said quietly, his voice full of genuine concern.

"I know," replied the younger man, his kind, sensitive gray eyes reflecting sadness. "He's like a second father to me, André, and I can't stand the thought of what this will do to him."

"But he knows what she's like—my God, Frederick, it'd be impossible for him *not* to know. The way she and Jacques were—"

"That may be true," Frederick interrupted gently, "but the fact is that, like it or not, she's his only child and he's made himself blind to the way she conducts herself. You know how important family honor is to him. But for his daughter to be pregnant and unmarried...well, I think you're right—it would kill him."

They sat in silence for a few moments, each one thinking how unstable the count's health had been these past few years since his heart attack. They knew they weren't being overly dramatic in their estimation of the effect the news would bring.

"If there were some way we could hide it from him till after the baby's born...." André said suddenly, his voice full of hope.

"I thought of that. I even asked her this morning if she'd consider going away. You know—tell him that she needs a rest after the trauma of the accident... needs time to get over Jacques's death."

"And what did she say?"

Frederick didn't answer immediately; he shifted his eyes down toward the marble tabletop and toyed with his wineglass for a few moments. Then he looked up slowly, his expression unreadable. "She said no. Refused absolutely. She has a 'better' idea."

André tilted his head in puzzlement. "You're going to think this is crazy—I thought so, too, at first. But then when I thought it over, it kind of made sense."

"*What* made sense?" André demanded.

Again Frederick fell silent for a few moments while he searched to find the right words.

"André, she wants *you* to marry her." He took a deep breath and prepared himself for the tirade that he expected to spill forth.

Oddly enough, his statement brought only a wry look of amusement to André's face.

"How convenient. How very, very convenient." André's voice was sardonic, his words clipped and terse.

"But if you stop and think about it for a minute, André, you'll see that her idea makes sense. If you marry her now—today—and then take her home and present Uncle Albert with a fait accompli—"

"The count isn't a fool, Frederick. Come on now!"

"I don't think it'll matter. Perhaps it'll be obvious what happened; perhaps not. But either way, she'll be married and the child will have a legal name. I think that's what will matter to him more than anything else."

André said nothing, and Frederick continued.

"It's not like you'd be doing it for *her*, anyway.

You'd be doing it for Uncle Albert. . . . Certainly you owe him something after all these years?"

André nodded and sighed heavily. "He's been like a father to me, too—you know that. He raised me, took care of me, gave me my education. But do you realize what you're asking me to do? My God, Frederick, I *detest* her! I'd be throwing away my whole life!"

"For my uncle's sake, I'd marry her myself—if she weren't my cousin," Frederick said quietly. "You know there's nothing I wouldn't do, if I could."

"But—marrying her!" André shuddered at the thought, and without realizing it he clenched his fists so tightly that his knuckles turned white.

Frederick grew thoughtful for a few minutes, then ventured, "She's always been in love with you, André. You know that. And maybe she'll try to be a good wife to you."

"Dammit, I don't *want* a wife! And if I did, it certainly wouldn't be her!"

Frederick leaned across the small table and gently placed a hand on André's forearm. "I know what you must be feeling. But if you don't marry her, you know what'll happen."

"She connived this whole thing!" André exploded, shaking his arm free of Frederick's grasp. "She never cared for Jacques at all. He was convenient for her, that's all. Ever since we were children she tried to seduce me, and when she realized that she hadn't a prayer of succeeding, she turned to him—thinking that if she couldn't have me, she'd settle for my younger brother."

"Jacques loved her, André, you know that,' Frederick said softly. "So even though we know what she's really like, at least she gave him some happiness until . . . the accident."

"Happiness!" André said with scorn. "You call that 'happiness'? She led him around by the nose and made sure he stayed as drunk and doped up as she was. And if you want to know the truth, I hold her responsible for his death."

"André!" Frederick said, shocked.

"Jacques was a decent person, an innocent kid who gave her his love, his adoration—his whole being. He wasn't a drinker—you know that. Yet, after a year of running around with her in Paris and Switzerland, he was an alcoholic and a—" He broke off, unable to continue.

"I know," Frederick said, wishing he could find some comforting words for André, who was like a brother to him. But there was nothing he could say. He knew the truth of what André had said, and there was no way he could refute it.

"I'll tell you something," André went on. "He was drunk when he went out that night—much too drunk to handle driving that car. And she knew it. And she let him go." His voice was bitter. "I think she *asked* him to go, knowing that the roads were covered with ice and that he was too drunk to drive a straight line, let alone try to maneuver down that winding mountain road."

Frederick said nothing. There was no way he could confirm or deny André's suspicions . . . he knew what a destructive woman his cousin was. It wouldn't be out of character for her to have done exactly what André had declared. When she wanted something, she would stop at nothing to get it. And she wanted André for her husband, not Jacques.

"That child will be my niece or nephew," André said reflectively. "Everything I am, I owe to the count; and I suppose I owe something to the unborn child, too. And to the memory of Jacques."

His broad shoulders sagged as if with a heavy burden, and he sighed deeply, with finality.

"Okay . . . I'll marry her," he said flatly.

Frederick's warm gray eyes were brimming with tears, and he made no effort to hide them.

"You're an honorable man," he said quietly, wishing that he could better express the enormous respect he held for him.

"But I'll tell you one thing—I'll never be her husband in anything more than name!" André promised, his rage surfacing again as he brought his fist down hard on the marble table.

"And I swear to God, Frederick, this is the last time she'll get her way. Where is she now?"

"In her hotel room," Frederick replied. "She already has the marriage license."

"How like her," André said angrily. "How typical! She was that sure of herself, eh?"

Frederick nodded, amazed at the machinations of his cousin.

But he comforted himself with the thought of how enraged and frustrated she'd be when she realized that André would never be more than a "pretend" husband.

Chapter 1

The swallows were circling overhead, their cries sharp as if they sensed the coming storm. The wind began to pick up, slowly at first, but within minutes turning into a howling gale. The trees swayed with the force, and as the new spring leaves were torn from their branches they danced through the air.

Janine looked up at the darkening sky, her expression anxious. She'd come so far to see the grotto, and to turn back now when she was so close seemed ridiculous. Besides, she reasoned, she could make it up to the cave and back again before the storm broke.

Parking her little Fiat at the foot of the steep incline, she glanced up at the narrow boulder-strewn path that wound upward to the cave. The climb would be difficult, she knew, and she felt a shiver of anticipation.

She had always wanted to visit Tours and the surrounding countryside, rich in art and literary history.

It was the land of Balzac and Rabelais, two of her favorite authors. Earlier that morning she'd visited Rabelais's birthplace in the town of Chinon, and then, when she would have started back to Paris, she realized that her excursion wouldn't be complete without a visit to the Grotte de la Sorcière.

In Rabelais's time, a sorceress famed for her powers of divination had made her cryptic prophecies in the grotto, and to Janine it was a place filled with the dark enticing mysteries of the supernatural.

Bracing herself for the onslaught of the wind, she opened the door of her car and stepped out. A violent gust engulfed her, whipping her shoulder-length auburn hair around her face. She jumped back into the car and fished through the glove compartment in search of a barrette; she would need both hands to keep her balance while she picked her way cautiously through the thorny bushes and craggy rocks, the last thing she needed was to have her hair in her eyes.

Fastening the barrette at the nape of her neck, she braced herself once more and stepped out of the car.

The wind was growing stronger every minute, and the low distant rumbles of thunder seemed to be getting closer. She took a deep breath to steady herself, then began to climb up the path, immediately regretting that she wasn't dressed properly. Jeans and a pair of sturdy hiking boots would certainly have been more appropriate than the thin gabardine pantsuit and sandals she was wearing.

Pitting her tall, slender body against the force of the wind, she made her way slowly up the path, carefully placing her feet to avoid twisting her ankles in the deep fissures that crisscrossed the rocks. Every few moments she stopped to breathe deeply, then climbed on, her eyes shifting again and again to the steadily darkening sky.

By the time she reached the top of the incline and saw the mouth of the cave, the rain had begun—big fat droplets that made a faint hissing sound as they struck the rocks every few seconds. She knew the downpour would follow in only a matter of minutes.

She turned and looked back down the path toward her car. There was no way she could make it all the way back down there in time; if she tried, she'd get drenched to the skin and her pale blue pantsuit would be ruined.

She glanced quickly at the opening to the cave. It was very dark and seemed enormous. She was standing at least ten feet from the entrance, but even at that distance the damp, musty smell of the cave seemed to envelop her.

It was a lonely place. There was no sign of human life anywhere around, save for a few little piles of charred wood left behind by last summer's campers. Taking in the whole scene, it was easy for Janine to picture the grotto as it had been ages ago, during the time of the famed sorceress.

Suddenly there was a loud deep rumble, then a violent crack of thunder, and the rain began to come down in torrents.

Instinctively she rushed for the protection of the cave, but once she was inside, a chill of fear began to snake along her spine. The hard-packed dirt floor glistened with moisture, and clumps of moss and lichen made eerie patterns along the smooth rock walls.

But Janine had never been one to give in to her fears. She settled herself on a broad rock ledge that jutted out from the east wall of the cave, and tried to calm herself as she prepared to wait out the storm.

Drawing her knees up to her chest and wrapping her arms around them, she huddled into herself for warmth, and rested her head on her arms. The steady rain had a soothing effect, and she allowed herself to take comfort from it. Then gradually she closed her eyes and drifted off into a kind of half sleep, feeling safe now in the womblike protection of the cave.

A sharp clap of thunder startled her awake, and her whole body twitched in reaction. She struggled to focus her eyes in the dim gloomy light, fighting that chill of fear she'd felt on entering the cave.

As if alerted by some sixth sense, she peered in the direction of the mouth of the cave. Her eyes grew wide with fright as she saw a tall man looming there, staring into the cave.

Terrified, knowing full well how isolated and vulnerable she was, she recoiled back against the smooth rock wall as if she wanted to melt into it, hoping that the man wouldn't see her.

But her movement caught his eye, and he began to walk slowly into the cave.

Every fiber of her being was tensed and her mind was racing frantically. To run toward the back of the cave where it was pitch dark would be stupid and dangerous; she'd be trapped. But she was trapped, anyway! There was no way out except back through the entrance, which was blocked by the man.

Her heart was pounding violently and beads of

perspiration lined her forehead. There was nothing she could do but wait; wait and see. . . .

"Excuse me, may I come in? It's really pouring out there!"

His voice was rich and deep and not at all menacing, but Janine was tensed with fright.

"Suit yourself," she said icily, hoping to convey a sense of confidence she was far from feeling.

The man approached, brushing the rain from the sleeves of his jacket as he came farther into the cave. He was so tall that he had to stoop slightly to avoid hitting his head on the ceiling of the cave.

"I hope I didn't frighten you," he said gently.

Janine looked up at him as he towered over her.

"I don't scare easily!" she snapped.

"Well, I just thought—you know, a young woman alone in a cave like this. . . ."

Janine felt some of her terror begin to ebb as she realized that he was trying to put her at ease. His smile was warm and his expression kind. Slowly she began to relax out of her tense coiled position.

"This rain. . ." she began, feeling more friendly toward this intruder.

"I don't suppose it'll let up for a while—April storms in this area usually last for hours." As he spoke he casually sat down beside her on the rock ledge.

She looked at the stranger more closely, realizing that he was extraordinarily handsome, with strong regular features and a deep cleft in his chin. His tweed suit was obviously expensive, and his fine leather loafers gleamed dully in the faint light of the cave.

Catching her look, he smiled and said, "I know this is awkward, but since we're going to be here for a while, will you tell me your name?"

She hesitated for an instant, still feeling somewhat wary, but as his smile broadened she felt reassured.

"Janine Aubry," she answered softly.

After an uncomfortable pause, he ventured, "I come here whenever I can. It's a good place to be alone, to think.... Rabelais's Panurge came here to consult the witch about his marriage plans...."

"And her predictions were less than encouraging!" Janine replied with a warm laugh, feeling much more relaxed now.

"Are you a fan of Rabelais?" she asked, certain that he must be since he was familiar with the story of Panurge.

"He's always been one of my favorite authors," the man said seriously, then smiled in that way that caused the cleft in his chin to deepen.

Janine felt the last vestiges of fear drain away.

She realized that he hadn't told her his name, and she was just about to ask when he took out a pack of cigarettes and offered her one.

"No, thank you, I don't smoke," she said.

He started to put the pack back in his pocket, but she reached out impulsively, lightly placing her hand on his wrist. "Please, go ahead. I like the smell of tobacco."

He eyed her skeptically for a moment, then pulled the pack out again and lighted a cigarette.

An enormous clap of thunder exploded outside the cave and she recoiled slightly. Then, feeling embarrassed, she said, "Having just told you that I don't scare easily, you'll probably think this is silly, but I'm terrified of thunder!"

"That's not silly at all. But we're perfectly safe in here," he said, glancing around the cave. "It's not the ideal place to spend a weekend, I grant you, but it's not all that bad."

Another explosion of thunder startled her, and he reached out to take her hand protectively in his. At first she drew away from his touch, but then relaxed and let him hold her hand, allowing herself to take comfort from the warmth of the physical contact.

"You're freezing!" he exclaimed, as her icy fingers lay close in the palm of his hand. Then he sized up her thin gabardine pantsuit and sandals, chiding her, "You're not dressed warmly enough!"

Releasing her hand abruptly, he stood up and whipped off his suit jacket. He leaned down and placed it over her shoulders, his dark wavy hair brushing against her cheek for an instant.

"Now you'll be cold!" she protested, trying to shrug her shoulders so that the jacket would slide off.

He placed his hands firmly on her shoulders and held her still. "But I'm dressed for the weather," he said teasingly, with a glance down at the white wool sweater vest he was wearing.

He sat down beside her on the rock ledge and put his arm around her shoulders. "You'll warm up soon," he promised, giving her a little squeeze.

They sat silently for a few minutes, listening to the sounds of the storm outside. It was almost dark out, as though the storm had brought the night with it, and it was raining harder than ever. Every few seconds it would let up, then come cascading down again with an angry roar. Occasionally a flash of lightning illuminated the inside of the cave, and each time Janine would observe her companion's face a little more closely.

In profile he was disturbingly handsome, his forehead high, his green eyes set deep, his chin prominent, with that little cleft in it that she liked more and more each time she looked at it. She tried to guess his age—thirty-five, perhaps, certainly not much older than that. She noted that he wore no wedding ring.

The lightning flashes gave him a chance to look at her more closely, too, though he was careful not to be obvious.

She was quite pretty, he thought, but there was something about her that was more compelling than merely an attractive face. He had a moment's impulse to run his fingertips along the graceful curve of her throat, but restrained himself. He didn't want to scare her, nor did he want her to know how strongly he desired her.

He knew she couldn't be much more than twenty-three, and he wondered briefly what she was doing here alone. She seemed, despite her fright when he'd first come into the cave, to be very poised and sure of herself. He detected a touch of sadness about her, too, and he wanted to ask her about it, but he said nothing.

The rain was like a curtain over the entrance to the cave, setting them apart from the outside and giving them both a feeling that they were in a tiny intimate world of their own.

Janine wondered why she felt so comfortable now with this man—a stranger, of whom she knew absolutely nothing, whose name she didn't know, but whose strong arm felt wonderfully secure and protective around her shoulders. She was surprised at her willingness to accept his casual embrace, for she was usually more reserved with men.

Perhaps it was just the strangeness of meeting him like this in the storm. The situation was so unusual, and she felt as though she'd been lifted out of the real world and transported to a dreamworld where nothing existed outside of the cave. It was an intoxicating sensation, and she made no effort to fight it.

The warmth of his body was soothing as she leaned more heavily against him, and she let her head drift down and to the side till it was resting on his shoulder.

"It's strange," he said softly, his deep voice blending with the sound of the rain on the rocks outside the cave, "meeting here like this. The rest of the world seems so far away. . . ."

At his words Janine gave an involuntary shiver. *The rest of the world. . . .* It was the last thing she wanted to hear right now, for it brought back the deadening remembrance of her life—her real life— back in Paris. She'd been away from it for only a week, but it seemed like ages, and she felt nothing but dread in the pit of her stomach as she thought about going home, going back to work.

As if he somehow sensed her feelings, he asked, "Can it really be all that bad?"

Janine nodded. "How did you know what I was thinking?" she asked in amazement.

"Oh, I don't know . . . perhaps being in the witch's

cave stirs up whatever E.S.P. powers I have." He laughed softly.

"Well, whatever the reason, you're right."

"About what, Janine?" he asked quietly.

"Oh, my life, my work—you know, all that stuff."

"You're much too young and beautiful to be bored with life already," he admonished tenderly.

"I'm just sick of it, that's all. The same boring routine day after day after day."

"What do you do?" he asked.

"I translate boring documents for a boring research company in Paris."

He laughed. "You make it sound like the tortures of the damned!"

"It is," she replied grimly. "I majored in languages in college, but my real love is history and genealogy. When I took the job I thought some of the material I'd be working on would be interesting, but it's not."

"Why not do something else, then? Surely it couldn't be that hard to find the kind of work you want."

She shrugged and turned her head slightly so that her face was half hidden against his chest.

"Let's not talk about it, okay? I don't want to think about tomorrow."

She wanted, suddenly, to tell him much, much more. Briefly, she shared with him the grief she still carried for her parents, who had died last year in a plane crash.

They had worked so hard all their lives to give her all that she'd wanted, and when they'd managed to save enough to send her off to the Sorbonne for her last two years of college, they'd been as happy and excited as she was. The plane had been bringing them from their home in Indiana to Paris for her graduation ceremony.

Janine told him what it had been like for her this past year in Paris, living alone, working at a job she hated, afraid to go back to Indiana because it would remind her of how happy her childhood had been and how desperately unhappy she was now. She poured out to him all the pain and loneliness that she had kept locked inside.

His arm tightened around her shoulders, drawing her closer and closer against him. The smell of his cologne lingered subtly in his soft woolen sweater vest, and she breathed it in, liking the masculine scent of it.

"You're very beautiful, Janine," he said softly, his lips so close to her ear that she could feel his breath.

With his free hand he tilted her chin so that he was looking down into her blue eyes, and he was startled to see that they were misted over with tears.

"I..." she began, but her voice broke off, and she tried to twist her face away, confused and alarmed by the rapidly building excitement she felt.

"It's like there's no one else in the world right now," he said, his voice deep and compelling. "No one and nothing...just the two of us, right now, in this cave...."

His eyes were soft and yet at the same time there was something very commanding about them. As his lips came closer and closer to hers, she shut off all the thoughts and judgments racing through her mind and gave in to the tender insistence of his lips.

It seemed as though the kiss lasted forever. Janine

had no concept of the passage of time, and as their mouths clung together, at first gently, then with growing passion, she felt more than ever that this must all be a dream...something quite apart from reality as she knew it.

Chapter 2

The birds were chattering noisily and the dull gray light of dawn was just beginning to filter into the cave. Janine awoke slowly and with difficulty, as if returning to consciousness was an enormous effort that required all her strength and will.

She was confused at first, not sure where she was or why. Then she remembered the storm . . . and the man. . . .

She jumped up off the rock ledge, gracefully stretched her long arms over her head, then began to rub the muscles at the base of her neck, which were aching horribly. She felt sore and cramped all over, and her pale blue pantsuit was creased.

She shook her head to clear away the cobwebs of sleep, and tried to think, to remember exactly what had happened. A hot rosy flush began to creep from her neck up to her cheeks.

Suddenly her legs felt too weak to support her, and she sat back down on the rock ledge. His jacket was lying neatly beside her, and she stared at it as if mesmerized, then began to run her fingertips over the rough tweed lapels.

After a few moments she pulled her hand away and ran her fingers through her thick, tangled auburn hair. Then she remembered that she'd been wearing a barrette; she'd fastened it at the nape of her neck to keep her hair out of her eyes while she climbed up the path. When had she taken off the barrette? She couldn't remember.

Her eyes darted toward the entrance to the cave. He was probably just outside, she thought. She opened her mouth to call out to him, then realized that she hadn't the slightest idea what his name was, and her voice died in her throat.

She combed her fingers through her hair once more, trying to tidy it as best she could, then walked out of the cave.

There was no sign of him anywhere. She searched the little grotto again and again, not wanting to believe that he had simply gone off and left her. She wanted to see him, to touch him, to feel the strength of his arms as he held her. . . .

Feeling lonely and abandoned, Janine returned to the cave and picked up his jacket, wondering why he had left it. Had he wanted her to have something of his so that she'd remember him? She smiled to herself. It wasn't likely that she'd forget, with or without the jacket.

She waited a short while, hoping that he'd return. But deep down inside she knew he wouldn't. When the sun began to creep over the horizon she wrapped his jacket around her and started to make her way back down the rocky path to her car.

The ground was saturated from the rainstorm, and by the time she reached her car her ankles were caked with mud. She tried to scrape it off with a twig she found in the roadway, but it was futile. She decided she'd have to stop at the first motel or restaurant she passed to get cleaned up.

She started the engine, then took one last look up the rock-strewn incline that led to the cave. Why had he left so mysteriously, she wondered, and where had he gone? She knew he must have arrived, and left, on foot, as there was no sign of another car having been parked in the thick mud of the little parking area.

Janine had always prided herself on her ability to think clearly and logically, to reason things out in an orderly manner, and the confusion she felt now was deeply troubling. It was as if the whole thing had been some kind of dream . . . and yet she knew it hadn't. The closeness she had felt toward the stranger had been a deeper and more meaningful emotion than anything she'd ever felt before.

Why had he left before she'd awakened? And why had he told her absolutely nothing about himself? The questions raced around and around in her mind, but she had no answers. She had only her memories, and his jacket.

The motor was running but Janine couldn't bring herself to shift into gear and drive away; couldn't resign herself to the fact that he had left without a trace.

She wondered if he had any idea how deeply he had touched her emotionally, and if he had felt anything at all for her beyond a casual attraction.

If only she had some clue to his identity, she could find him—somehow. . . .

But would he want her to?

Her eyes misted over as she remembered how they had talked late into the night, sharing their thoughts and feelings. Yet, every time she had asked him anything specific about his life, he had dodged, hesitated, changed the subject.

Unconsciously she was running her fingertips along the lapels of the jacket as she stared out through the windshield, seeing nothing, lost in her thoughts.

Then suddenly she dug her fingers frantically into the jacket pockets, thinking that perhaps she might find something, some piece of identification. . . .

But there was nothing. . . nothing in the front pockets. . . nothing in the outside breast pocket. . . nothing. . . .

And then her fingers curled tightly around a thick piece of paper, and she drew it slowly out of the inside breast pocket.

It was a photograph, in vivid color, of a pond or small lake, with a few white swans gliding majestically across its mirrorlike surface, their graceful necks arched high. There were feathery-looking willow trees along the far shore, and a dilapidated wooden pier or platform of some kind that sloped down into the water. In the foreground stood the man, dressed in casual brown slacks and beige pullover sweater, his dark hair slightly windblown, the cleft in his chin very striking as he smiled into the camera.

Janine studied the picture for a few moments, then put it back in the pocket and laid the jacket neatly beside her on the seat. The photograph told her nothing—it could have been taken anywhere, at any time;

it was just a lake, somewhere—yet she felt oddly comforted by it. She would never know who he was, but at least she could look at his picture whenever she wanted to, and relive the moments she had shared with him.

She shifted into gear and pulled her car out onto the Paris-bound highway, not quite sure how she felt, or why, but determined not to think right now, not to feel. . . .

THE APRIL SKY was brilliant and the city sparkled like a jewel beneath it. Janine thought she had never seen Paris look lovelier. The flower stalls that dotted the street corners were loaded down with daffodils and lilacs, and the new spring fashions were displayed elegantly in the windows of the designers' shops.

The sunshine felt warm and golden on her shoulders as she walked, quickly and with an air of determination, toward the office of the agency for which she worked. She'd made a few decisions since yesterday morning when she'd left the grotto, with the picture of the stranger tucked away in the inside pocket of his tweed jacket.

She was amazed at the way she felt now, only twenty-four hours later. Instead of being depressed because she would never see him again, nor ever even know his name, she felt elated, delighted, and more hopeful than she'd felt since the death of her parents.

Driving back to Paris, Janine had realized there were two ways in which she could deal with the situation: she could continue to mope or she could remember all the things the man had said to her—all the new thoughts and feelings he'd stirred within her—and she could act on them and begin to take her life in a new direction. The encounter in the cave had given her an enormous amount of energy, and she could turn that energy into positive or negative action—that was her choice to make.

There was a decided bounce to her step as she climbed the narrow stairway of the office building and walked into the reception area of the agency.

Yvette, the receptionist, for whom Janine had an enormous fondness and warmth, looked up as she entered.

"Well, look at you!" Yvette's large dark eyes sparkled. "You're positively radiant! What happened on your vacation?" Her voice dropped to a whisper as she asked the question.

Janine laughed heartily. "Wouldn't you like to know!" Her blue eyes twinkled mischievously, and her full lips curved into a smile.

"A man—that's all it could be!" Yvette decided firmly, nodding her head of tiny black curls. "You met a man."

Blushing, her smile broadening, Janine shook her head no. "Why do you always think that when anything good happens to a woman, a man has to be involved?"

But Janine knew the answer. Yvette was a hopeless romantic; she fell madly, deeply in love at least twice a month, and believed that love and romance were the only worthwhile things in the world.

"You cannot tell me I'm wrong," Yvette remarked as she scrutinized Janine's rosy flush and happy smile. "One look at your face is all I need. It's obvious."

Her pronouncement made, Yvette leaned forward across her desk to get a closer look at her friend.

"Absolutely," she said with conviction, nodding again. "Now, tell me all about him."

"Yvette, you're hopeless!" Janine exclaimed with a laugh. "There was no man. I went to Tours and Chinon, visited some of the local historical sites, saw Rabelais's birthplace...I even stopped at the Grotte de la Sorcière—that's the place where Panurge consulted the—"

"But there was a man. I can tell. Where did you meet him?"

Janine laughed again and shook her head. "You think you're clairvoyant, but you're wrong."

She couldn't have said why she wouldn't talk about it. Perhaps she was afraid that if she told Yvette, she'd start to feel sad and lonely again, instead of feeling this new strength and determination. Or perhaps it was simply that she didn't have the right words to really express what had happened that night in the cave.

"But," Yvette persisted, "I can always tell. You know how? By your blush. When I'm in love I always blush."

"Yes, and you're always in love! If you wouldn't fall in love with every man you met, maybe you'd learn what real love is all about," Janine remarked, hoping that the seriousness of her tone wouldn't offend her friend.

She dearly loved Yvette, yet sometimes she wished she could take her by the shoulders and give her a good hard shake to make her understand that there was more to life than men, men and more men! But

Yvette was incurable, and Janine's frequent lectures fell on deaf ears.

"Real love—false love," Yvette shrugged her narrow shoulders, "love is all that counts. There's no 'real' or 'false' about it. There's just love." And with that she sighed contentedly.

"Oh, why do I bother?" Janine exclaimed, shaking her head in mock resignation. "We're never going to see eye-to-eye on this."

"And what does Bernard have to say about this new man?" Yvette asked suddenly, arching her delicate eyebrows.

Janine's flush grew deeper. Bernard! She hadn't thought about him even once while she'd been away. She'd been dating him for a few months, and though she liked him very much, that was as far as her feelings for him went—much to his displeasure. Bernard was hopelessly head over heels in love with her, and had vowed to wait until Janine returned his love, which he was sure wouldn't be too long.

"Well, did you tell him?" Yvette prompted.

"Tell him what? There was no man." Janine's eyes were still twinkling mischievously. "And even if there had been, I wouldn't want to talk about it—to anyone!"

Janine had begun to walk past Yvette's desk toward the door to her boss's office, but she stopped suddenly and turned back to her friend.

"I'm going to give him my resignation today," she said with conviction.

"What?" Yvette exclaimed. "But why—"

"I've given it a lot of thought," Janine cut in, her tone serious now. "I hate this kind of work—you know that. It bores me to death. And I'm tired of Paris. I'm tired of everything I've been doing this past year.... And I'm tired of the way Bernard keeps mooning around after me with that hangdog look on his face."

"But, Janine! He's in love with you!" Yvette defended him, as if that explained everything and made it all right.

"But I'm not in love with him," Janine replied firmly. "And I'm not going to be, either. Despite what he thinks."

Yvette shook her head in dismay. "You Americans!" was all she could say. "You understand nothing of the beauty of the chase, the pursuit, when a man and a woman—"

"Enough!" Janine cried, holding up her hand. "My decision is made."

"The only thing that could've brought this on is meeting another man. I knew it." Yvette's excitement bubbled forth. "Oh, Janine! Tell me all about him! What's he like? Is he very handsome? Is he—"

"Yvette, please. I said I don't want to talk about it—and I mean it."

"All right, I'll stop," Yvette agreed. "No more questions."

"Thank you," Janine said simply, feeling greatly relieved.

"But what are you going to do? Do you have another job lined up?" Yvette asked.

"I stopped by a few newspaper offices before coming in this morning," Janine replied. "I put ads in—to see if I can get some free-lance work."

"Translations?" Yvette asked.

"No. I'm sick of doing that. I want to do genealogical tracings."

Yvette wrinkled her nose. "What a thing to be
interested in! You want to spend your time researching other people's family histories? That sounds more
boring than translations!" She shook her head again,
and her black curls bobbed gently with the movement.

"Well, you're interested in men, I'm interested in
history! To each his own, as they say," Janine
replied. "Besides, it might be a chance for me to get
out of Paris.... I put in the ads that I'm willing to
travel practically anywhere in Europe."

"But Paris is the best city in the world!" Yvette
cried in protest, truly baffled now. Why anyone
would choose to leave Paris, especially in the springtime, was far beyond her powers of comprehension.

She didn't know what else to say. Obviously something of great magnitude had happened to her friend
during her vacation. And obviously she wasn't going
to talk about it. So there was nothing Yvette could
say or do to persuade Janine otherwise.

"I hope you find whatever it is you're looking for,"
she said softly.

"Thanks, Yvette. I hope so, too. I don't know what
it is, but I know it isn't here in Paris."

She straightened her shoulders, tossed her thick
auburn waves, and walked directly into her boss's office, not bothering to knock.

Chapter 3

The next two weeks dragged by as Janine experienced deeper and deeper doubts about the wisdom of having quit her job so hastily. She'd received only a few replies to her ads, and none of them seemed to offer what she was looking for. But her money was beginning to dwindle and she realized that she'd have to accept one of the offers very soon, whether it "sounded right" or not.

Every morning she ran down the five flights of stairs to the lobby of the little pension where she rented her apartment, and anxiously opened her mailbox, hoping to find an offer of an interesting job. And each morning she climbed slowly back up the stairs, and sat in her tiny two-room studio, wondering what in the world she was going to do now.

On her dressing table, encased in a small gold-fluted frame, was the picture she'd found in the man's jacket. She stared at if often through the long boring afternoons, drawing comfort from it, telling herself that she was indeed doing the right thing—that he would be glad she was making this change in her life. Hadn't he told her to find the kind of work that really interested her? Hadn't he said that she was much too young and beautiful to be bored with life already?

She would just have to be patient—as patient as time and finances would allow. She wouldn't think about the future but would concentrate only on to-day, and tomorrow, looking forward to the delivery of each morning's mail.

She had broken off with Bernard a week before and felt very sure it was the right decision. After having experienced such closeness with the man in the cave, she knew she couldn't accept a relationship with a man who really didn't interest her. To go on seeing Bernard now, after knowing what it was like to feel so drawn to and in harmony with another man, seemed like the worst sort of hypocrisy. She felt badly that Bernard had been hurt, but there was nothing she could do about that; however, she felt strong twinges of guilt each afternoon when the florist's delivery boy knocked at her door and hand-ed her a single long-stemmed rose with a note that read: "I love you. What happened?"

Finally as the third week began and she was grow-ing desperate she received the response to one of her ads that she'd been waiting for. Janine couldn't ex-plain to herself why this particular offer interested her while the others didn't, but she accepted what her intuition told her, and sent off a cable saying that she was delighted to accept the job and would arrive at Weisdorf Castle in one week.

She had always wanted to explore Bavaria, and the

thought of being in a castle high in the Bavarian Alps, researching the family of Count Albert von Erlich, seemed fantastically exciting to her.

"Sounds deadly!" was Yvette's comment when Janine called her to say that she'd be leaving Paris first thing tomorrow morning.

"Well, not to me!" Janine replied with a laugh. "I understand from his letter that his family archives are quite extensive. And I looked on a map this morning and discovered that the castle is situated in one of the most beautiful parts of the country. It's near Ober-ammergau, and there are lots of castles in that area that I've always wanted to see. I'd love to explore those fairy-tale castles built by Ludwig the Second."

Yvette simply couldn't understand why Janine would want to go off exploring castles built by a mad king, when she could just as easily stay in Paris and meet lots of men. She said so, quite bluntly, but Janine's enthusiasm wasn't dampened.

"I just know that this is what I have to do right now," she said. "Trust me—I know it sounds crazy, but I have a feeling that I have to change my life drastically, and this is my chance. I might not get another one."

As DAWN BROKE dully over the city Janine crammed the last of her suitcases into her little Fiat. She'd told her concierge to go ahead and rent the apartment to someone else; she wouldn't be returning.

Standing now in the doorway and taking one last look around the tiny two rooms in which she'd spent the last year of her life, she felt as if an enormous burden was being lifted from her shoulders; the relief of it made her feel like she was soaring through the air free as a bird.

Dressed comfortably in faded blue jeans that hugged her slender hips, and an old green cashmere sweater, with her thick auburn hair pulled back and tied with a green satin ribbon, Janine looked much younger than her twenty-four years. And for the first time in longer than she could remember she felt young and alive, eager for whatever experiences were waiting for her out there in the world.

She pulled the apartment door shut and walked quickly down the five flights of stairs to her Fiat parked at the curb in front of the little pension. Her blue eyes misted over as she glanced at her shoulder bag lying beside her on the front seat; tucked away inside it was the photograph. . . .

As she shifted into gear and headed out of the city she realized that the picture was the only thing she possessed that really mattered to her. With it she felt strong and sure of herself, as if the man reminded her of her own vitality and connection to life.

CROSSING THE VOSGES MOUNTAINS of northeastern France, Janine felt filled with excitement. It was only a few miles now to the German border and the Bavarian Alps. The mountainous terrain was new to Janine and she found it breathtakingly beautiful. The craggy peaks towered against the clear blue sky, their lush green slopes dotted with pines and firs, and she had glimpses of spotted deer grazing peacefully in the sunshine.

Lower down in the valleys, spring was well under way, and there were wildflowers everywhere.

Patches of bright pastel colors peeked out from hollows in rocks and among gnarled old tree roots as far as the eye could see.

The skiing season was over and it would be a few weeks before the first of the summer tourists arrived, so she had the roads almost entirely to herself. Janine loved this kind of driving, as her car held its own on the hairpin turns that wound around the mountains.

The air at this altitude was both relaxing and invigorating, and she opened all the windows of her Fiat, then pulled the satin ribbon out of her hair, feeling gloriously alive and happy.

As night approached, the blue of the sky changed to rose and violet, the mountain peaks loomed dark and rather menacing, and the tall firs began to cast eerie shadows over the land. There was a kind of mysterious compelling beauty to it, and Janine felt deeply moved. She stopped her car at the side of the road several times just to sit silently and absorb the extraordinary atmosphere.

She had no itinerary nor did she feel any need to make one now. She would sleep—when it suited her—at inexpensive inns or motels.

After spending her first night at Lindau, on Lake Constance, where the pleasure boats ferried back and forth between Germany, Austria, and Switzerland, she set off again through the mountains. There were many small villages dotting the alpine slopes, the small low houses huddled together, their red-tile roofs projecting far from the walls for protection against the winter snows.

She loved the curious rock formations that loomed above the mountain roads. Once she looked up and

saw a series of craggy rocks that folded in upon themselves, looking like angry waves on a storm-tossed
sea. Firs grew in long lines along the crests of the rock
waves, which seemed to have been caught at the
height of their fury, frozen forever into strange tormented shapes. And emerging here and there from the
rock waves were the rounded, bulbous church towers
typical of the region.

Before going on to her job at Weisdorf, there were
two castles that Janine particularly wanted to see.
Both had been inhabited by Ludwig II of Bavaria,
who, even if he was as mad as history claimed, had
been a highly unusual person—a man with a keen political sense, a passion for art, and enough of a grasp
of science to create dream castles that still remained
the envy of architects and engineers the world over.

She was rather disappointed when she reached
Hohenschwangau, for it was a castle of conventional
Gothic construction; it was solid and dignified but
not nearly as impressive as she'd hoped.

However, when she drove on to Neuschwanstein,
she found a true fairy-tale castle fit for Cinderella or
Sleeping Beauty, and she was filled with delight.

Ludwig II had been an intimate friend and loyal
patron of Richard Wagner and had dedicated this
marvelous castle to him. Janine was awed as she
toured the rooms, each one decorated to evoke a
different scene from the great composer's many
operas.

Gazing out through the high narrow windows,
Janine remembered reading how much Ludwig II had
loved the mountains, the lakes and streams that
could be viewed from the castle, and how on snowy

winter nights he rode his golden sleigh across the plains below.

As she and the rest of the small tour group followed the guide from room to sumptuous room she listened attentively to the details about the life of this unfortunate king, who had lived only three months in the castle that had taken him many years to build. Pursued by political enemies who intended to have him committed to an insane asylum, he had chosen suicide by drowning rather than allow himself to be stripped of his freedom and his dignity.

Janine was struck by the recurring motif of swans. They appeared everywhere in the castle—carved into ceilings and bedposts, painted on walls, woven into cushions and tapestries. Ludwig had had a passion for the graceful birds, for they recalled his favorite Germanic legend—the tale of Lohengrin, a knight who was aided by a swan—and he had ordered the swan motif to be used throughout the castle.

Again, Janine was strongly reminded of the man in the cave. In the photograph she could clearly see the swans gliding across the lake behind him. . . .

She wished that he could be here with her now, sharing this fascinating experience. Unconsciously she hugged her shoulder bag a little closer to her side, knowing that the picture was safe inside, tucked away in its little gold-fluted frame.

Dusk was settling as she pulled into the little town that lay nestled at the foot of the mountain where Weisdorf Castle was situated. It was a charmingly picturesque place, and Janine wished the daylight would linger long enough for her to look around, but it was almost dark now—and besides, she would need the entire evening to get herself ready for tomorrow when she had to present herself at the castle.

She checked into the town's only inn—a tiny place with accommodation for no more than eight people at the most—and ran herself a hot bath immediately.

She changed into a clean pair of comfortable jeans and loose sweater, then took a long hard look at herself in the full-length mirror on the bathroom door.

She would need every second available between now and tomorrow morning to transform herself from a dishevelled-looking American girl into a dignified-looking young career woman fresh from Paris.

She scrutinized her face closely, realizing that in the five days since she'd left Paris, she hadn't once put on so much as a trace of lipstick!

Running her fingers through her tangled auburn waves, she piled her hair high on top of her head, and twisted her full lips into what she hoped was a very sophisticated expression. But the effect only made her burst out laughing.

There was time enough tomorrow morning, she decided. Right now she felt young and carefree and full of excitement about the new life she was carving out for herself.

Chapter 4

After the gloriously sunny weather that had lasted throughout Janine's trip through the Alps, it was raining hard when she reached Weisdorf Castle. The road leading up to it rose steeply, full of twists and turns, and her little Fiat had to exert all its power to make the climb.

Perched on the very summit of the mountain the castle seemed typically Gothic in construction, with towers and crenellations and long narrow windows. The rain darkened the gray stones of the outer walls, giving the whole place a somber melancholy appearance.

She left her car parked under an imposing portico at the base of a huge stone stairway that led up to the main entrance. Luckily she'd taken her umbrella out of her luggage this morning, for without it she would have got soaked to the skin.

Janine climbed the stairs as quickly as she could, and looked with wonder at the huge wooden door with its iron studs and crossbars. To the left of the door was a bell mounted on the stone wall. As she pressed it, she heard a buzzer go off somewhere deep inside the castle.

She glanced down and took one last look at her outfit. The beige linen skirt and matching jacket were very conservative, the chocolate-brown satin blouse beneath added just the right touch of contrast without being gaudy, and the narrow gold choke chain at her throat was simple and elegant. She'd tried a few different hairstyles this morning before deciding to let it cascade softly to her shoulders. The only makeup she wore was a trace of eyeshadow, which made her eyes appear a startling robin's-egg blue. The overall effect was soft and subdued, but very businesslike.

She knew her appearance this morning was of the utmost importance, because she had to inspire trust and confidence in her new employer. While she hadn't exactly lied in her ads, she had worded them so that they would give the impression that she was a bit older and more experienced than she actually was.

Finally, after what seemed an interminable length of time, the heavy wooden door opened just a crack and an elderly woman with steel-gray hair poked her head out.

Startled, Janine jumped back a step, then managed a smile.

"Hello. I'm Janine Aubry. Count von Erlich is expecting me."

"Yes," came the terse reply as the woman opened the door a little wider but made no move to step back and let Janine enter.

She was dressed entirely in black and had sharp thin features. As she gave Janine the once-over, her face hardened.

Uncomfortable under the woman's gaze, Janine repeated, "Count von Erlich is expecting me."

Finally the woman stepped back a few inches to allow Janine to enter, but she had to twist sideways to do so without bumping into her.

Janine found herself in an enormous entrance hall that was impressive because of its size but somber because the high narrow windows didn't let in enough light. There were mirrors mounted on the doors that opened off the hall, and they brightened it a little as they caught and reflected the inadequate light from above. Heavy wooden tables with gold inlays lined the gray stone walls, and here and there were benches with elaborately carved legs. At the far end of the hall a golden statue of Cupid holding a lamp marked the foot of a curved staircase.

The atmosphere was cold, gloomy, and damp, and Janine shivered a little.

"Please sit down," the woman said, indicating one of the benches, and Janine had the distinct impression that it was a command, not an invitation.

Probably just a nasty old housekeeper, she mused to herself as she sat on the bench the woman had directed her to.

Her black silk dress rustling softly, the woman left the hall, and Janine sat and waited. And waited.

She was just beginning to wonder if the woman had neglected to inform the count of her arrival, when one of the mirror-covered doors opened and two men came into the hall.

It was easy to guess which one was the count, Janine decided. Tall and thin and slightly stooped, he looked to be in his mid-sixties. His face was deeply lined, and the style of his white mustache was definitely old-fashioned. From behind his thick rimless glasses, his eyes were a pale blue. There was a fringe of white hair around his head just above his ears; otherwise he was nearly bald. There was something about him that made Janine think he'd seen many sorrows in his lifetime.

The other man, however, seemed just the opposite. He couldn't have been more than a year or two older than Janine, and with his curly blond hair and easy smile he seemed out-of-place in the grim austere atmosphere of the castle.

The older man stepped forward and bowed with old-world courtesy, then held out his bony hand and clasped Janine's warmly.

"It's a pleasure to meet you, Miss Aubry, and to welcome you to Weisdorf. I'm Count von Erlich, and this is my nephew, Frederick Rheinberg." As he spoke he nodded toward the younger man.

Breaking into a dazzling grin, Frederick attempted a formal bow similar to the one his uncle had just given, then laughed deeply and said, "Hello!"

Janine instantly thought of Yvette, who would have fallen madly in love at the sight of this curly headed youth.

"Did you have an enjoyable trip?" the count asked in a formal voice.

"Very enjoyable, thank you," Janine answered just as formally, not quite sure how to react to this unlikely uncle-nephew team, but feeling relieved to discover that the housekeeper wasn't typical of the inhabitants of the castle.

"You drove all the way?" the count asked conversationally as he took her elbow and began to lead her down the hall toward the curved stone staircase.

"Yes, I took the 'student's route,'" Janine replied. "I couldn't pass up the opportunity to visit Hohenschwangau and Neuschwanstein. What an extraordinary place Neuschwanstein is!"

The count smiled and nodded in agreement. "Ludwig the Second has been much maligned through the ages, I'm afraid. But he left behind such exceptionally beautiful monuments—and in spite of his extravagances and obsessions, I believe he was loved by his people."

Janine smiled warmly, feeling certain that she could learn a great deal from the count. "I understand he was an ardent patriot who was fiercely proud of his Bavarian heritage. It's not hard to understand why the idea of his kingdom being joined to that of Prussia was so abhorrent to him."

"I'm glad you have some familiarity with the subject, Miss Aubry," the count remarked as they came to a halt at the foot of the stairs. "You see, that's what your job here is all about. I believe my family is in some way linked to his, and I want you to study the records to determine just what the connection is."

Janine couldn't repress her excitement and a smile lighted up her face. "It sounds fascinating—just the kind of work I was hoping to find!" she exclaimed enthusiastically.

The count peered at her over the top of his spectacles. "I expected you to be . . . well, a bit older, Miss Aubry."

Apparently her youth—and perhaps her good looks—had caught him off guard.

"Well, I think it's a delightful surprise," Frederick cut in, much to Janine's relief.

He flashed her another dazzling smile and stepped forward to take her arm.

Count von Erlich nibbled nervously at the tip of his mustache as he continued to look her over, and Janine had the impression that her presence was somehow disturbing to him. She was sure she'd dressed correctly for the occasion, and she couldn't imagine what it was that he seemed to be inwardly debating.

Then he waved his hand abruptly and muttered, "Well, it doesn't matter."

Whatever his doubts were, apparently they were now laid to rest, and he resumed his role as gracious host.

"You must be very tired, Miss Aubry. I'm sure you'd like to freshen up after your journey. Emma will show you to your room. I trust you'll find it satisfactory; if not, please feel free to request whatever you require."

Janine was about to say that she wasn't tired at all, but then she thought better of it. She was eager to see her room; and besides, so far everything was completely different from what she'd expected. She wanted a chance to sit and think about it.

"Please take your time getting settled in," the count went on. "There's plenty of time before luncheon, after which I'll show you the library and the archives."

He pushed a button set into the stone wall and Janine heard a bell ring somewhere in the distance. Because so much of the castle was stone, it echoed eerily.

Within seconds the old woman who had opened the front door appeared at the other end of the hall and began to walk toward them.

Janine tried to smile warmly in response to the woman's scowling expression, but her efforts fell somewhat short.

"Emma, please show Miss Aubry to her room," the count instructed, "and make sure she has everything she needs."

"Yes, sir," she said with a quick nod that made Janine think of the way an eagle would move its head.

Then, turning to Janine with that same birdlike nod, she snapped, "This way, please!" and began to walk smartly up the stairs.

"But—my car—my luggage...?" Janine asked quickly.

Emma halted in mid stride. "You car has been parked and your luggage is already in your room. Please come!" she repeated with greater insistence.

Baffled, Janine began to climb the stairs behind her.

The count muttered something, then disappeared through another of the mirror-covered doors. Frederick followed close on his heels, but at the last moment he turned around and gave Janine a big wink.

She had to hurry to catch up with Emma, who had already rounded the first landing and was climbing the second flight.

"Your room is on the third floor," she called over her shoulder. "You'll have to get used to the climb, if you plan to stay here."

"Oh, that's no problem! I don't mind stairs!" Janine replied as Emma's back disappeared around the second-story landing.

Janine was panting by the time she reached the third floor, for each flight seemed the length of three normal ones, and she marveled at the fact that Emma, who was at least in her sixties and rather heavy, appeared quite unruffled by the exertion.

"Gosh, that's quite a climb! You must be in terrific shape," Janine said with a little laugh, hoping to find her way into the housekeeper's good graces.

Emma, however, seemed to take no notice of Janine's attempt at friendliness. Her face remained taut, her expression severe.

She turned abruptly and marched off down the hall, and Janine, watching her from behind, had to suppress a chuckle. Emma waddled as she marched stiffly along, and with her broad hips and short stature, Janine thought she looked like a dumpy toy soldier. To add to the ludicrous picture she made, her gray hair was pulled back into such a tight bun that it made her head look too small for her pear-shaped body.

Emma stopped short in front of a door far down at the other end of the long corridor, then stood there waiting until Janine caught up, at which point she threw open the door.

Again, Janine had to maneuver sideways to get past her and enter the room. And then she just stood there, overwhelmed.

The bed—an enormous four-poster affair with a heavy brocade canopy—stood in the exact center of the room, facing three diamond-paned casement windows. One entire wall was taken up by a massive closet made of solid, heavy mahogany. On the wall adjacent to it were two matching mahogany bureaus with intricately carved gold handles on the drawers. Above the bureaus hung a gilt-framed mirror that looked like it weighed close to a ton.

Emma proceeded to open a door on the far side of the room and Janine trotted along behind her.

"This is your bathroom," she explained. Janine craned her neck and peered in.

It was old-fashioned but its elegance couldn't be disputed. The enormous tub stood a few inches off the floor, supported by short iron legs that were shaped like claws, and the faucets were gold. The floor and sink were made of beautifully veined green marble. Apparently the count had made one concession to modern plumbing—the toilet; sleek and oval-shaped, it was low to the floor and looked brand new.

Emma briskly turned on all the water taps, then shut them off, as if to demonstrate that everything worked perfectly. Then she returned to the bedroom and opened the huge doors of the mahogany closet.

"Your suitcases are in here," she said pointedly.

Then she simply stood there, her feet planted firmly in the thick sculpted carpet, her hands on her hips.

"Thank you, Emma," Janine said, not knowing what else there was to say at this point.

Emma made no move, and Janine looked at her quizzically. What in the world did this strange woman want?

She had planned to begin unpacking right away, but Emma apparently wasn't going to budge from the spot where she was standing, which was directly in front of the closet.

When some seconds had passed and it became obvious that no move on Emma's part was forthcoming, Janine ventured in a hesitant voice, "Excuse me, but I'd like to unpack now. You're standing in my way."

Emma gave that weird birdlike nod and moved precisely one step to the left.

Frustrated, Janine still had to sidle past her to get to the open closet.

She hauled her suitcases out, then pushed them across the room and began to lay her neatly folded garments out on the bed, trying to create some order before stowing them in the bureau drawers and hanging her dresses in the closet.

All the time she was doing this she could feel Emma's eyes on her. At first she'd thought Emma was going to help her unpack, but obviously the woman had no intention of doing so. She stayed right where she was, her hands on her hips, watching Janine.

Finally Janine straightened up and turned to face her.

"Is there something you want, Emma?"

"Please be as quiet as you can. Frau Karla is resting and must not be disturbed!" She glared at Janine as she spoke.

"Who's Frau Karla?" Janine asked in surprise.

"She is the daughter of Count von Erlich—the mistress of Weisdorf!" Emma pronounced in an imperious tone.

"Very well, Emma. I'll be as quiet as I can," Janine answered politely. "I certainly wouldn't want to disturb Frau Karla."

"See that you don't!" Emma commanded, then strode out of the room, almost slamming the door behind her.

When everything was unpacked and put away, Janine opened up her shoulder bag and took out the photograph of the man she'd met in the cave. Funny . . . it seemed like ages ago, but it had been only a few weeks.

Carrying the gold-fluted frame in her hand, she went to the window and looked out. The rain had stopped but a strong wind had kicked up, and dark clouds were scudding across the gray sky. She could see mountaintops in the distance, but only intermittently as the clouds obscured them, then cleared for a second or two and folded in again. A light mist smoothed out the landscape below, filling in the hollows and ravines, and there was a strange perfect stillness about the view. There were no signs of life in the valley directly below her windows, and if there were any animals grazing on the hillsides Janine couldn't see them.

She looked back at the photograph, wishing that somehow she could tell him what was happening in her life now—about the bold adventurous steps she'd taken because somehow he'd given her the courage and inspiration to change her life.

She wanted to laugh with him again, and to feel the warmth of his embrace.

But she shook herself out of her reverie, remembering she had a job to start, and her new employer was waiting for her. Quickly washing her hands and face and running a comb through her hair, she dashed out of her room and was halfway down to the second floor when she realized that she hadn't put the photograph away.

She ran back up to her room, grabbed the picture from where she'd left it on the windowsill, and replaced it in her shoulder bag. Then she hid the bag under a pile of sweaters in one of the bureau drawers. She had toyed briefly with the idea of leaving it out on the nightstand beside her bed, but then she'd felt funny about it. This wasn't her home—she was merely an employee here—and somehow the picture seemed to her too intimate to be displayed where strangers might come upon it.

Chapter 5

Once again Janine found herself seated on a bench in the gloomy entrance hall. She had no idea where luncheon was to be served, and she didn't think it would be appropriate to go wandering around in search of the right room, so she just sat there waiting, hoping someone would come to fetch her.

Suddenly a door opened and into the hall stepped a young pretty girl wearing a lace cap and matching apron over a red gingham dress.

"Miss Aubry? I'm Hilda," she said with a smile that illuminated her blue eyes. "The count asked me to show you in to lunch."

Janine stood up, returning the girl's warm smile. There was something sweet and gentle about her rosy-cheeked face, and Janine decided immediately that she liked her—and what a refreshing change from that awful old housekeeper!

She followed Hilda through yet another of the mirror-covered doors and found a pleasant surprise.

The room was small and cozy, and quite unlike what she'd seen of the other rooms in the castle for it was furnished with light airy pieces, and the oval glass-and-chrome dining table was very modern.

The count and his nephew got to their feet as she entered, and waited for her to sit down before they resumed their places.

"I trust everything was to your satisfaction?" the count asked agreeably, referring to her room upstairs.

"Oh, yes, everything's fine," Janine replied. "But it's all so—so enormous!" She took another look around the cozy little dining room and added, "Not at all like this!"

The count shook his head sadly. "I love the old baroque style, but Frederick makes me keep up with the times—at least in this room."

Frederick laughed and said teasingly, "If I had my way, I'd tear down the castle and build a long low house, with Picassos on the walls, indoor pools, and Japanese landscaping."

At which the the count groaned and shook his head, and they all laughed.

At that moment an elderly man dressed in a butler's black tuxedo came through the door at the other end of the room, pushing a serving cart before him.

He had a hawklike face and was somber and silent as he quickly performed his duties then disappeared back through the door.

Frederick had been watching Janine's bewildered expression during this curious performance. "Don't worry about old Hans—he's harmless enough. He only looks scary; that's his defense against that old hag he's married to!"

"Frederick, that's neither kind nor fair," the count chided, but his tone was something less than serious. Then he turned to Janine and added, "Hans and Emma have been with my family for many, many years."

So, Hans was Emma's husband, Janine thought. Well, certainly that alone would account for his grim expression.

The meal proceeded pleasantly, with Frederick teasing the count and the count pretending to be angry but obviously enjoying his company immensely. Janine was happily surprised at the food—chicken breasts in white wine with mushrooms, and a crisp endive salad—for she'd expected, and dreaded, the typically heavy German fare.

Janine was dying to ask the count about his daughter Karla, but since she hadn't appeared at luncheon and the count hadn't brought up her name even once, she thought it would be best to wait until later. Still, she thought it odd that Karla, since she was "mistress of Weisdorf," hadn't yet welcomed her to the castle.

However, she did learn a bit about the count's nephew, Frederick, whose disarming good looks were beginning to get to her; she couldn't help grinning back at him every time their eyes met. He explained that he'd just finished law school and was clerking for a law firm in Munich while awaiting the results of his bar exams. He spent as much time as he could at the castle, and it was clear that he and the count were very close.

Janine decided that Hans the butler either had

E.S.P. or had been spying through the door, which had been left slightly ajar, for the moment she finished eating and put down her fork, he appeared silently at her side to remove her plate.

"Coffee, sir?" he asked in a deep resonant voice, and the count nodded, then looked at Janine.

"Please," she replied.

Hans and the serving cart disappeared through the door, then returned a moment later. As he stood behind and slightly to her left, the gleaming silver coffeepot in his hand, she heard him breathing deeply, as if he had asthma.

Janine shifted her slender shoulders a little to the right, to give him room to pour the coffee into her cup. She had the distinct impression that he hesitated for a split second before beginning to pour.

"*Ohhh!*" she cried, jumping up out of her chair. Her beige linen skirt was covered with scalding hot coffee.

"Please excuse me, Miss. I'm terribly sorry," Hans mumbled, and continued apologizing as he bowed his way backward out of the room.

"Please accept my deepest apologies, Miss Aubry," the count said earnestly, rising to take her arm. "Hans is old, and perhaps his eyesight isn't what it used to be. Are you all right?"

Janine nodded. "I—I think so."

"I know this is a terrible inconvenience," the count continued, ushering her out to the hall, "but if you'll give your clothes to Emma she'll see that they're returned to you as good as new. And take your time changing," he added. "Frederick and I will wait for you in the library. Hilda will show you the way."

Back up in her room Janine changed quickly into a charcoal-gray velour pantsuit that seemed to match the moody weather. She tried hard not to make a big deal out of the incident with the coffee; tried to assure herself that the count had been right—Hans's eyesight probably was failing.

In any case her skirt had absorbed most of the hot coffee, and while her thighs felt uncomfortably hot, she really hadn't been burned.

But she couldn't help remembering the way Hans had hesitated before beginning to pour. For some reason she suspected he'd done it deliberately.

Whether or not it had been an accident, one thing was apparent—Emma and her husband certainly weren't going out of their way to make her feel welcome here.

But the count was a kindly old man, and Frederick's sense of humor had already helped make her feel at home in these strange surroundings.

HILDA LED JANINE through a maze of rooms, all baroquely furnished, then out to a stone corridor. Their footsteps echoed strangely, and Janine decided that this must be the oldest part of the castle.

Every now and then Hilda turned back and smiled at her, and Janine felt more and more at ease with the young girl.

"Hilda," she ventured. "How many people live here?"

"Well, let's see... there's Count von Erlich, of course, and Frau Karla, and Mr. Rheinberg—although he's not here all the time—and there are five of us who work here. Six actually, if you count my sister Ursula, but she left last year to get married."

"So far I've only met Hans and Emma," Janine remarked, hoping that this would prompt Hilda to divulge some information about the peculiar old couple.

Hilda wrinkled her nose and said, "Emma runs the place with an iron hand. She raised Frau Karla, and she thinks that gives her the right to order the rest of us around."

Janine thought that this explained Emma's authoritarian attitude, but it did nothing to help her understand Emma's animosity toward her. She noted, however, that both Hilda and Emma referred to the count's daughter as "Frau" Karla, which meant that she was married, yet neither of them had mentioned her husband.

Janine was just about to question Hilda about this when she came to a halt in front of a heavy wooden door with wrought-iron fittings, and knocked.

"Come in!" called the count, his voice muffled through the thick door.

Hilda opened the door for Janine, then smiled at her and walked off down the long stone corridor.

Janine entered the library and stopped short. She'd been awed by the size of her bedroom, but it was tiny compared to this! The vaulted ceiling was two stories high, and at the far end of the room was an oak staircase that spiraled up one flight to a gallery that circled the entire room. The walls were completely covered with books.

The count and Frederick were seated at a long wooden table about halfway down the room, and she walked toward them with wide-eyed amazement.

She'd never imagined that a private collection could be so vast.

With his usual courtesy, the count stood up as she reached the table. "I hope you'll enjoy working here," he offered, directing her to a chair next to Frederick.

"Oh, I'm sure I will!" Janine responded enthusiastically. "I've never seen anything like this—outside of museums and libraries."

"Please feel free to explore the collection and make use of whatever interests you. However you'll find that the most important literature isn't among these books."

He pulled a key out of his vest pocket, unlocked one of the cupboards on the wall behind the table, and brought out a number of coarse linen sacks, each about the size of a pillowcase. Then he untied the drawstring of one of the sacks and dumped its contents onto the table.

There were papers and manuscripts of all sorts and sizes—bits of parchment, journals and letters tied up with ribbons, and yellowed envelopes whose old wax seals were broken and crumbling.

"These are typical of the documents you'll be working on," the count said, resuming his seat. "One of your tasks will be to draw up a list of any and all documents pertaining to my family history. We have connections with France dating back to the seventeenth century—which is why I responded to your ad: I need someone who is equally fluent in French and German."

"Actually, I'm the one who first saw your ad," Frederick interrupted, with that beguiling smile of his. "And I'm certainly glad I did!" With that he winked at Janine, and she blushed hotly.

The count peered first at Frederick, then at Janine, his pale blue eyes twinkling behind his rimless spectacles. Then he cleared his throat and continued, "It's especially important that you research any links that may have existed between the von Erlichs and the Wittelsbachs."

Janine knew this last name. It belonged to one of Bavaria's most illustrious families—a family that had supplied the country with many dukes and kings during the period when, with the aid of France, the Bavarian monarchy was first established. It would indeed be a connection to be proud of, and Janine was sure that family pride was a matter of the utmost importance to the count.

"My wife, the Countess von Erlich, was a Lansfeld," the count said, looking at Janine as though he expected some reaction to this revelation. When there was none, he shifted his gaze down to the table.

Janine had noticed that he referred to his wife in the past tense, confirming her suspicion that he was a widower. Perhaps that explained the sadness she'd detected when she'd first met him this morning.

"When I was younger," the count went on, "I was very much tied up with my business affairs and had little time to devote to my family history. In fact, to tell you the truth, I wasn't even very interested in it. But one's interests change as one gets older, and now this genealogical research is almost an obsession with me. Unfortunately I haven't the expertise required to do it myself."

Janine understood what he was trying to say, and

she felt a surge of warmth toward the old man. "I'll do my best, Count von Erlich. But I'm afraid it may take me quite a long time, since your records are so extensive."

The count shrugged. "Time's not the important thing. It's accuracy. I only hope you won't find the work too tedious."

"Tedious?" Janine laughed softly. "Quite the contrary—I'm sure I'll find it fascinating!"

"All the same, we're hidden away in a very remote part of the country, and I'm sure that after the gaieties of Paris you'll find it very dull here. The nearest village is about ten miles away, but it's a quiet place. For anything more exciting you'll have to go to Munich, and I urge you to do so whenever you wish."

"That's very generous of you, sir, but I'd much rather explore the countryside around the castle. It's so beautiful here!"

"You can walk for miles and miles and never leave Weisdorf," the count said with pride. "And I'm sure that Frederick will be delighted to show you around."

"'Delighted' is certainly an understatement," Frederick replied, and gave Janine a look that she couldn't possibly misunderstand.

"That would be wonderful," she mumbled. "Perhaps—"

"How about right now?" Frederick asked eagerly. "I could show you the lake and the—"

"I think Miss Aubry might like to rest now," the count said firmly.

"But I have to go back to Munich first thing in the morning," his nephew said, "so—"

The count's look silenced him; but after a second Frederick's warm smile returned, and he said to Janine, "I'll be back in a few days."

"Dinner will be served in the formal dining room at eight o'clock," the count said, as he drew out his gold pocket watch and glanced at it. "That gives you a few hours to relax, and to think over what we've been discussing. If you have any questions about your work, we can discuss it over dinner."

With that he snapped the Florentine case of his watch and slipped it back into his pocket.

JANINE LAY ON THE BED staring up at the heavy brocade canopy. The man in the cave had never been far from her thoughts during the afternoon, but now it was almost as if he were here beside her; in her mind she was talking to him, telling him how excited she felt at the prospect of the fascinating work ahead.

During the few weeks since their encounter in the cave, she'd relived every moment of it over and over again, savoring every detail, recalling the sound of his deep rich voice, and the feel of his strong arms around her.

Suddenly her thoughts shifted to Frederick. She knew it was ridiculous, because she'd never see the stranger again, but somehow she wanted to apologize to him for feeling attracted to Frederick. His curly blond hair and twinkly gray eyes, coupled with his sense of humor and wit, delighted her.

She laughed to herself as she thought of what Yvette would say if she could see her now. Yvette would probably tell her to make a play for Frederick, to do anything she could to draw him to her side, make him fall in love with her.

But really, Janine reflected, there was nothing she had to do. It was obvious that Frederick was already quite taken with her.

He was no match for the stranger in the cave, but he was definitely attractive and she liked the thought of spending time with him. She had her work to occupy her days, and perhaps Frederick would occupy some of her evenings. . . .

The knock on her door startled her out of her reverie.

"Yes?" she called.

"Miss Aubry? Dinner's in an hour," Hilda announced through the closed door, then walked off down the long hall.

Chapter 6

The formal dining room was on the same scale as everything else in the castle—immense. But Janine was beginning to feel more comfortable now, and she wasn't quite so overwhelmed by the cold heavy feeling of the stone walls and the enormous wooden furniture.

"What can I offer you, Miss Aubry?" the count asked. "Whiskey? Or perhaps a glass of sherry?"

"Sherry, please," Janine replied.

The count was standing at the far end of the room, in front of a mahogany sideboard where he was pouring out drinks from cut-crystal decanters. Frederick was standing beside him, and as Janine glanced at them she was struck again by the odd contrast. The count wore a formal three-piece suit, a carnation on the lapel, and with his fringe of white hair and his thick rimless spectacles, he looked something out of the nineteenth century. Frederick, however, looked the epitome of modern youth. His gray

French gabardine slacks were snug around the hips, the top button of his white dress shirt was unbuttoned—giving him a casual but elegant look—and his curly blond hair just brushed his collar.

Because the count dressed so formally while Frederick seemed to prefer more casual attire, it had taken Janine quite a long time to select what she thought would be an appropriate outfit to wear for dinner. She'd finally decided on a white knee-length skirt with a kelly-green silk blouse that made her auburn hair look startlingly red.

Frederick's eyes lighted up as he took his seat next to her at the table, and she was sure she'd made the right choice.

"To your new job, and your welcome presence among us!" Frederick said, lifting his whiskey glass in a toast.

Janine smiled warmly at him and began to sip her sherry. She was admiring the elegant crystal glass, and was about to comment on it, when suddenly both the count and Frederick turned their heads toward the doorway.

Janine followed their glance.

There stood a most unusually clad but devastatingly beautiful woman. Janine guessed her to be about thirty, but it was hard to tell, because her face was so thickly covered with makeup.

"Karla!" Frederick exclaimed with a note of mockery in his voice. "To what do we owe the pleasure...?"

The woman waved her hand imperiously and proceeded to walk slowly into the room.

"I wasn't aware that I needed a special invitation,"

she said cuttingly as she gracefully lowered herself
into a chair directly across the table from Janine.

Janine was stunned. So this was the count's daughter, the mysterious Frau Karla.

There was no doubt that she was extraordinarily
beautiful, but somehow the expression on her face was
almost ugly. Her dark eyes were lined with thick
iridescent turquoise shadow, and her raven-black hair
was pulled back into a very severe knot at the nape of
her neck. Both her eyes and her hair gleamed dully in
the light of the chandeliers over the table. Her black
floor-length evening gown was so low-cut and revealing that Janine felt embarrassed and looked away.

The count seemed to be on the verge of saying
something, and several times he opened his mouth,
then closed it again.

Karla was now glaring directly at Janine, who had
the uneasy feeling that somehow she was being chal-
lenged by her, but she had no idea why.

She looked helplessly at the count, and he cleared
his throat nervously.

"Miss Aubry, may I present my daughter, Karla."
Then he turned to Karla. "Miss Aubry is the researcher I told you about. She's here to dig through
the archives and determine the nature of our family
connection with Ludwig the Second."

Karla's face was completely blank as she received
this news. She stared at her father but seemed not to
see him, as if she were looking through him to some
distant spot on the wall behind his chair.

Again the count cleared his throat. "I hope you'll
make Miss Aubry feel welcome and at home among
us," he said.

Karla turned her head slowly and looked at Janine. "Delighted," she said with an ill-concealed lack of enthusiasm.

Janine couldn't help noticing how little she resembled her father, and decided that her dark eyes and hair must have come from her mother's side of the family.

"Pleased to meet you," Janine said softly, lowering her gaze. She wasn't sure why, but she felt very uncomfortable looking directly into Karla's face.

"Are you enjoying your stay at Weisdorf, Miss Aubry?" Karla asked.

"Yes, very much, thank you. I'm..." Janine's voice trailed off, as Karla, obviously not in the least interested in her reply, turned toward Frederick.

"You don't mind, dear cousin?" she asked sarcastically as her long thin arm snaked across the table to snatch up Frederick's glass of whiskey.

She took a long deep swallow, then set the glass down on the linen tablecloth in front of her and began to toy with it, turning it around and around very slowly, her diamond bracelets twinkling and sparkling hypnotically in the soft light of the chandeliers.

"How lovely you look tonight, Karla," Frederick said mockingly. "One would have thought, judging by your modest gown, that you were off to a nightclub."

Ignoring him, Karla took another long swallow of whiskey and turned back to Janine.

"Are you enjoying your stay at Weisdorf, Miss Aubry?" she repeated. Apparently she'd forgotten that she'd just asked this question.

Janine was more than a little puzzled, but she decided that whatever was going on she'd best pretend not to notice it.

"Yes, very much, thank you," she replied.

"Then I envy you," Karla said abruptly, with yet another deep swallow of whiskey. She set the glass back down on the table, and Janine noticed that her fingers were trembling slightly. "I'm bored to death in this place!" she snapped.

The count smiled nervously, as though trying to conceal his embarrassment.

"Please, Karla! If you take that tone, it'll be less than encouraging for Miss Aubry."

"*Dear* father, I'm quite certain that Miss Aubry didn't come here to rifle through stacks of dusty old letters day after day by her own choice. If she were free to do as she wished, she'd have picked a more interesting place than this. What's the point in pretending otherwise?"

She reached for the whiskey glass and drained it. Then in a scathing voice she continued, "You may as well know, Miss Aubry, that this 'research' of my father's is a total waste of your time and his!"

Frederick had gone to the sideboard to pour himself another glass of whiskey to replace the one Karla had taken from him, and had returned to the table just in time to hear the end of Karla's tirade.

"That'll be just enough, cousin," he said, his voice like steel, quickly noting the count's pained expression.

At that moment Hans appeared and began to serve the meal. Janine was greatly relieved for this break in the tense conversation, and she attempted to lighten the mood by exclaiming delightedly over the fresh trout amandine and asparagus soufflé.

It was a meal she would have enjoyed immensely under any other circumstances; but now her heart wasn't in it, and everything tasted like cardboard.

The dinner proceeded in awkward silence with the count and Frederick exchanging glances every few minutes while Karla sat there moodily, closely scrutinizing Janine. Janine noticed that she'd once again relieved Frederick of his glass of whiskey and, having finished it, had told Hans to bring her the bottle. Her plate of food lay untouched, and she continued the process of draining the glass and refilling it every few minutes.

By the time Hans began to clear away the plates, Janine had lost count of how many drinks the woman had had. Karla's face was very flushed and the strange glazed look in her dark eyes was even more pronounced.

Janine, remembering all too clearly how Hans had poured the scalding coffee into her lap at luncheon, refused the offer of coffee after dinner. She was just about to attempt to excuse herself from the table, to escape to the peace and quiet of her room, when Karla suddenly lit into her.

"What do you do to your hair?" she demanded in an aggressive tone, her voice thick and heavy from drinking.

Taken aback Janine replied, "Nothing...nothing in particular. I just wash it and set it."

Karla let out a shrill laugh. "Who are you kidding?"

"I don't dye it, if that's what you mean," Janine

said, beginning to feel angry. She'd done nothing to provoke this attack, and she was getting tired of trying to be courteous in response to Karla's hostility.

Karla started to say something, but Frederick cut in quickly, "If she says it's her natural color, then that's what it is. Now lay off, Karla. I mean it!"

Karla gave him a look full of malice. "Men are such suckers—so easy to fool. And we all know that American girls are expert in that department."

With that she gave Janine a menacing look, then rose abruptly and flounced out of the room.

After she'd left there was a tense embarrassed silence for some moments before the count said quietly, "I must ask you to forgive my daughter's behavior, Miss Aubry. I'm afraid she's been anything but welcoming toward you."

"Please don't trouble yourself over it, sir," Janine replied. "It isn't important."

"You see, she's in rather poor health, and, quite frankly, I think she takes far too many tranquilizers than are good for her."

And far too much whiskey, too, Janine thought, but of course she didn't say so out loud. There was no need to embarrass the count any further.

"My wife suffered a long lingering illness before she died," the old man continued, his pale blue eyes misting over. "She wasn't well enough to look after Karla properly. In fact it was Emma who really brought her up. She was like a second mother to her—and Emma adores her so much that she's never been able to refuse her anything. I'm afraid it hasn't always been good for Karla to have her every whim satisfied."

He paused for a moment before he went on, "I've made a few mistakes where Karla is concerned. She's my only child...and sometimes it's hard to know what's best—whether to be strict or indulgent."

"I understand," Janine said softly, feeling sorry and embarrassed for the count. "But please don't feel that you have to explain or apologize to me for anything."

"All I'm really trying to say, Miss Aubry, is that I hope you won't take what she says too seriously or allow yourself to be hurt by it," he finished, looking sad and very tired.

"Please, don't worry about it, sir. I'm here to do a job, not to become your daughter's best friend. If she wishes to be rude to me, I'll just ignore it."

Apparently Frederick thought more explanation was in order, and he added, "Karla's very hard to predict, so don't be lulled into a false sense of security with her. She can be warm and friendly one minute— then turn around and bite your head off two seconds later! So don't be fooled when she suddenly becomes all sweetness and light, Janine."

Janine noticed that he'd made a point of calling her by her first name, and she smiled warmly at him in response. It seemed to her that by addressing her so familiarly he was establishing a bond between them, a friendship, and she was pleased by it.

Apparently the count hadn't failed to notice the way his nephew had addressed her. He looked from Frederick to Janine, then back again to Frederick, but he said nothing. However Janine saw the hint of a smile that played at the edges of his mouth.

"I think, too, that she's just plain bored—and lonely," Frederick went on. "Her husband's away on business almost all the time, and I think that gets on her nerves."

This was the first mention of Karla's husband, and Janine was filled with curiosity. What sort of man could he be? And if Karla had always been as strange and unpleasant as she was now.... Janine desperately wanted to learn more about Karla, but she knew it wasn't her place to ask.

"If she's so bored perhaps she should try to get out once in a while...drive to Munich..." Janine ventured.

The count let out a deep heavy sigh. "She used to do that from time to time, but nothing good ever came of it," he said, then lowered his head in embarrassment or grief, Janine couldn't tell which.

She tried to guess what he was implying. Scandalous behavior? Lost drunken weekends? It didn't seem unlikely.

Now there was a hushed silence in the dining room, and the rain outside made a soft hissing sound as it hit the windows.

"Would you like to hear some music?" Frederick asked suddenly.

Janine nodded. "I'd like that very much."

Having said good-night to the count, who remained at the table to finish his coffee, Frederick led Janine across the hall and into a salon that was much smaller than she'd expected.

She immediately noticed the harp and the piano that stood side by side in front of the window. Frederick, following her glanced, quickly asked, "Do you play?"

Janine laughed. "No, but I wish I did. They're both such beautiful instruments."

"What would you like to hear?" he asked as he led her to a long low bookcase that was filled with albums.

"Something soft and soothing," Janine replied.

Frederick gave her a curious smile, then pulled out an album and put it on the stereo.

They settled down on a satin-upholstered sofa near the stereo, and Janine leaned back against the cushions, sighing inaudibly. The strains of Beethoven's Fifth filled her ears, and she began to feel the tension from dinner drain out of her.

She was glad to be here alone with Frederick and felt very grateful to him. His warm smile and constant attention definitely helped make up for Emma's cold reception and Karla's hostility. His presence made her feel less alone, less vulnerable in this vast cold castle.

Chapter 7

The following morning Frederick left the castle just after sunrise, but before he went he slipped a note under Janine's door. She saw it lying on the carpet as soon as she woke up, and tore open the envelope eagerly.

> Dear Janine: I wish I could really express how much I enjoyed meeting you. I have to be in Munich at least till the middle of next week, but I'll be thinking of you while I'm away. Try not to let Karla get to you—don't let her nastiness infect your sweet disposition and marvelous sense of humor. I'll be looking forward to seeing you as soon as I get back.
>
> Affectionately, Frederick

Janine knew she would miss him during the coming week. He was one of the those warm outgoing people who have the knack of creating a pleasant congenial atmosphere wherever they go, and now the castle seemed empty without him.

The first few days passed quickly, however, as she began to delve into her work, familiarizing herself with all the details that she would later have to examine minutely. She found the work absorbing and was thankful for it—it left her little time to daydream about the stranger in the cave or to count the days until Frederick was due back.

By now she had met all the household servants and had found them all to be as warm and friendly as Hilda—with the exception, of course, of Hans and Emma. Hans continued to hover over her at mealtimes, his asthmatic breathing sounding loud and annoying in her ears. She watched him closely, trying to determine if his eyesight was failing as the count had claimed, but found no evidence of it. He seemed to see as well as anyone, which affirmed her suspicion that he'd poured the scalding coffee into her lap deliberately. The only reason she could come up with was that Emma must have told him to do whatever he could to make her uncomfortable.

Emma....

Janine shuddered. The wretched old woman was growing colder day by day, to the point where she wouldn't even acknowledge Janine's presence. Whenever Janine needed anything, Hilda took care of it. Clearly, Emma had refused to have anything to do with her.

It was becoming increasingly evident that Emma's feelings for Karla bordered on worship. She doted on her to such an extent that she seemed even to take on Karla's feelings as her own—and since Karla obviously was determined to be as unpleasant as possible to Janine, Emma did the same.

Janine had given the matter considerable thought, wondering why Karla should dislike her so. Karla had come downstairs for dinner only once since Frederick had left, and at that time she'd made a point of ridiculing Janine's interest in her work, had openly criticized her clothes and her hairstyle, and had made several unpleasant remarks about American girls in general. Janine had tried to control her anger, pretending not to have heard the caustic comments.

Other than that, Janine's encounters with Karla had been wordless, but just as disagreeable. Occasionally she would run into her in the corridors or the large entrance hall. At those times Karla would look down her nose at Janine as though she were a servant and needed to be reminded of her position. Janine always tried to smile, to be friendly, but her efforts were futile. Karla would refuse even to call her by her name, merely nodding her head curtly when Janine greeted her.

It seemed to her that in some obscure way Karla felt threatened by her. Perhaps it was merely that Janine was young and extremely pretty, with her large blue eyes and thick auburn hair, and to Karla that somehow represented competition. But what, Janine wondered, could she possibly compete for? Karla was mistress of the castle, and she was merely an employee of the count.

It was quite baffling, and would have been very upsetting if she hadn't had her work to keep her so occupied. Still she wished Frederick would return soon. While he might not be able to explain why

Karla and Emma disliked her, he would at least be good company, and his warm smile and sense of humor would make her feel comfortable.

The count had left her pretty much to herself in the library all week as she sorted through the ancient letters and journals, and she saw him only at mealtimes. He was always charming and pleasant, and eager to know how her research was coming along. She didn't have much to tell him yet, because she hadn't finished arranging the documents into chronological order. But she assured him that she was finding it interesting, and he seemed pleased to hear it.

She longed to question him about Karla, but since he avoided mentioning her at all, she felt it wise to hold back her questions until Frederick returned. However, the more she observed the strange goings-on in the castle, the more curious she felt.

Occasionally she would catch a glimpse of Karla wandering like a ghost along the corridors upstairs. She was always dressed lavishly in chiffon or satin negligees and always wore very heavy makeup. Diamonds and emeralds glittered in her ears, on her fingers and around her wrists.

Janine had no idea where Karla's room was situated, but she often saw Emma trotting down the hallways, laden with trays of food and whiskey. It struck her as odd that Emma loved Karla so much but apparently didn't mind contributing to her drinking problem.

Drinking problem . . . .

Janine was growing more and more certain that drinking was only the bare beginning of Karla's problems.

Two nights before Frederick was due to return Karla put in another appearance at dinner. This time she wore a vivid red cocktail dress, knee-length, with a matching ostrich-feather boa draped dramatically around her shoulders. However, the boa did nothing to conceal the décolletage of the dress, which was so revealing that Janine wondered how the count could even look in her direction without blushing.

She wondered, too, how Karla could stand to be so scantily clad when the cold dampness of the castle seemed to reach deep into Janine's bones. Perhaps all the liquor she consumed kept her warm, Janine reflected. In any case, although the rain had let up a few days ago, the castle still felt drafty and chilly, and Janine had given up on skirts and dresses altogether in favor of turtleneck sweaters and woolen slacks.

The meal progressed much as Janine expected it would—unpleasantly. After consuming nearly an entire bottle of Scotch and accusing Janine of trying to make her feel uncomfortable in her own home, Karla stormed out of the room. Apparently she'd been provoked by something Janine had said, but Janine had no idea what it might be. She thought briefly of how Frederick had said that his cousin could be very sweet and charming; if that was so, she certainly hadn't seen any evidence of it so far.

She was wondering how the count could put up with such rudeness and aggression from his only child when he cleared his throat and said, "I expect she'll be calming down soon. André is due back tomorrow or the next day."

André? That must be her husband, Janine decided.

In as casual and uninterested a voice as she could manage, she probed, "Is that Frau Karla's husband?"

The count nodded. "A wonderful man, André. He's away on business most of the time, but when he's here Karla's like a delighted child."

"André is a French name, isn't it?" Janine asked, knowing already that it was. She was merely trying to find questions that might prompt the count to divulge more information.

"Yes," he replied, nodding again. "André Gerard is his full name. I was very close to André's parents before they died. At that time André and his younger brother, Jacques, were just children, and when they were left orphans I decided to take them in and raise them myself."

Janine listened intently, hoping the count would go on. Perhaps somewhere in the description of Karla's husband would lie the explanation for his wife's obvious problems.

"So Karla and her husband were both raised here at the castle?" Janine prompted.

"Well, yes, in a manner of speaking. Of course, André is seven years older than Karla, so they had little in common during their childhood. But Jacques was close to Karla's age, and as children they spent a great deal of time together. He was very much in love with her."

The count paused, and his face took on an expression of infinite sadness.

"I loved those boys as though they were my own," he said quietly. "Jacques was killed three years ago in an automobile accident in Switzerland."

Again he fell silent, and for a few moments he seemed lost in thought.

"And then André and Karla married very suddenly, just a month or so after Jacques's death. André's business keeps him away more than Karla would like," the count added. "She feels lonely and cooped up here, and often I feel guilty about it and wish it were possible for her to get out once in a while. Unfortunately both her husband and her doctor feel it would be unwise for her to leave.... Of course, she could at least go out around the grounds and take walks, but she seems to prefer to stay in her room by herself, with only Emma for company."

He shook his head sadly.

"Well, she'll cheer up as soon as her husband arrives," he said. "It's really too bad that he has to be away so much—it's so hard on her!"

"She must love him very much," Janine remarked.

"Yes, she does," the count said. "But from my own experience, I know how it is when a man starts becoming very successful—sometimes he feels he must devote almost every minute of his time to his career. In a way it becomes like a child to him, and all he wants is to nurture it, see it grow."

"What business is he in?" Janine asked, unable now to restrain her inquisitiveness.

"Automobiles," the count replied. "When he and Karla married, André owned one Mercedes dealership in Paris. Now, however, after only three years, he owns two in Paris, one in Brussels, and one in Amsterdam. And," the count added with obvious pride, "he's been so successful that now he's begun branching out even more. He's added a whole new line of expensive American cars to his Mercedes line."

"That's quite impressive, sir," Janine said, knowing that the count expected her to praise his son-in-law. "But I can understand how hard it must be for Karla. While it's wonderful to have a husband whose career is successful, it must be hard, too. Perhaps...well, perhaps that's why Karla drinks so much and takes so many tranquilizers. Maybe she just can't stand the pain of missing her husband."

The count nodded gravely. "I think you're right, Miss Aubry. But, of course, there are other factors...."

He fell silent again, and Janine knew better than to pursue the conversation any further.

THE NEXT DAY the count appeared at Janine's side in the library just before lunchtime.

"Aren't you beginning to find this all a bit tedious?" he asked with fatherly concern.

"Not at all, sir," Janine assured him.

"Well, you've been at it almost nonstop for over a week now, and I wish you'd take a break. I wouldn't want to be accused of overworking you," he added with a playful smile. "Why don't you take the afternoon off and go exploring around the grounds? The weather's beautiful today, and I think the fresh air would do you good."

"Well, perhaps I will," Janine replied, thinking how delightful it would be to smell the sweet mountain air instead of the stale mustiness of the ancient documents.

But a part of her wanted to stay right where she

was, surrounded by countless stacks of yellowed
papers. She was finding the job more and more interesting every day. Delving into the count's family
history was like taking a journey back through time,
back into the unknown. The bundles of letters tied
with faded ribbons beckoned to her, whispering of
adventure and romance in times past. And now it
was almost time to begin untying those ribbons and
prying into the secrets of the past; she had just this
morning finished setting up her filing system and arranging the bundles in chronological order.

Well, perhaps the count was right—perhaps she
did need a break. She decided that she would do as
he'd suggested and take the afternoon off. And
tomorrow she would begin what she knew would be
the most interesting, intriguing part of her job—the
reading of the letters and journals.

She thanked the count quickly, and ran upstairs to
her room to change. Jeans and a sturdy pair of walking shoes seemed a good choice, and at the last
minute she added a heavy cable-knit beige pullover
sweater, then fastened her thick auburn hair with a
silver barrette at the nape of her neck.

It was indeed a beautiful afternoon. The sun shone
brightly from an incredibly blue cloudless sky, and
the surrounding mountain peaks glistened with the
last remains of their winter covering of snow. Lower
down on the slopes stood tall russet-hued beech trees,
and still lower down, where the grass grew thick and
green, she could see cows and sheep grazing contentedly.

Janine circled the castle, finding it even larger than
she'd assumed it to be, and then discovered at the

western side of it an enormous, beautifully tended rose garden.

She walked through the garden for a while, stopping to smell the delicate fragrance of the buds, which were just now beginning to open, before she saw the path. It began at the end of the symmetrically laid out flower beds and seemed to lead into wilder territory, where nature took over.

Intrigued, Janine decided to follow it.

Chapter 8

She could have followed any of the little paths that branched off the one she was on—shady walks that wound beneath the trees in every direction—but she was afraid of getting lost. Besides, the main path was so beautiful with thick lush vegetation encroaching from all sides. Her ears were filled with the bubbling gurgling sounds of hidden mountain streams, and the air was redolent with the fragrance of evergreens.

She rounded a bend and suddenly found herself face to face with a strange-looking man dressed in typical Bavarian fashion—a green jacket with leather breeches, and a green felt hat that had a long curving feather angling out from it. He was much shorter than she, and she had to look down to see his face, which was partially concealed by the brim of the hat.

"Oh, excuse me!" she said, stepping back a little way. "I was just exploring the . . . ."

She hesitated, suddenly noticing the double-barreled shotgun that he carried over his shoulder. By his side was an enormous German shepherd that was snarling and growling deep in its throat.

"Does he bite?" she asked nervously as the dog began to circle her, sniffing at her ankles.

The man shook his head no but still said nothing.

"Well, if you'll excuse me," Janine said, hoping the man would move out of her way so she could continue on down the path.

But he stood his ground.

"Going to the lake?" he asked gruffly.

"Oh, is there a lake at the end of the path?" Janine asked. "This is my first time out, and—"

Abruptly, the man snapped a command at his dog, then whirled around and set off down the path in the opposite direction.

How creepy, Janine thought, and gave a little shudder. Well, he was probably just a gamekeeper or something like that, she assured herself, continuing on her way, curious to see the lake he had mentioned.

When she reached it, she stopped and stood stockstill.

There were a few swans gliding lazily and gracefully across the surface. There were willow trees along the far shore, and a dilapidated wooden pier sloping down into the water.

Could it be . . . ?

No, of course not, she told herself firmly. There had to be hundreds of little lakes like this all over Europe.

And yet the more she looked, the more sure she felt.

This was the lake where the photograph had been taken—the one of the marvelous stranger she'd met in the cave! She felt something like a cold chill creeping along her spine, and goosebumps covered her skin.

She'd stared at the photograph so many times that every detail of it was engraved in her mind's eye, and she knew that she couldn't possibly be mistaken. This *was* the lake.

She stood gazing at the scene for several minutes before she spotted the rowboat tied to the wooden pier.

In the photograph there hadn't been any boat. Of course, the boat could have been elsewhere on the lake the day the picture had been taken.

The logical, practical side of her mind insisted that she was wrong, that this couldn't possibly be the same lake—what were the odds against stumbling upon the very lake where the man had had his picture taken? Probably five thousand to one, she mused.

But the emotional, intuitive side of her mind insisted with equal determination that this definitely was the same lake. It wasn't just that everything looked exactly as it did in the picture—even the tiny details, like the way one of the willow trees bent down at nearly a right angle to touch the water; it was more than that. She tried to find the words to express what it was that made her so certain, but she could find none.

The two conflicting parts of her mind argued back and forth, practical against emotional, and finally she didn't know what to think. She could only stand there, amazed, shaken, wondering if perhaps her mind was playing tricks on her.

"There you are!"

She whirled around like a creature possessed, not sure who had spoken—or indeed if anyone had.... She could see no one.

Then there was a movement in the bushes behind her, and out stepped Frederick, his warm gray eyes twinkling with delight, a grin spreading across his face.

"Oh, you startled me!" She sighed heavily with relief.

He joined her on the lakeshore and casually slipped his arm around her shoulder as if he'd done so a hundred times before.

"I just got back. Ernst told me you were down here," he said, giving her a little squeeze.

"That funny-looking little man I met on the path? He really gave me a scare when I ran into him!"

He hugged her even closer to his side.

"I've missed you, Janine," he said, and there was no way she could have misinterpreted the tone in his voice.

She laughed hesitantly, trying to hide how shaken she felt.

"I missed you, too," she said.

"Is something wrong?" Frederick asked, looking searchingly into her face. "You're as white as a ghost!"

"No... nothing—really. It—it's just that man I met on the path, I guess. He really gave me the creeps."

It wasn't what she wanted to say. She was thinking of the man in the cave, and the photograph, and her feeling that this was the lake where he'd been standing. . . .

But she couldn't tell him—couldn't tell anyone. She knew it would sound ridiculous, and, apart from that, it was an extremely private matter.

"Don't let him upset you," Frederick said as he sat down on the sandy shore, then reached up to grab her hand and gently pull her down beside him. "He's just as harmless as Hans—in fact he's Hans's brother. His job is to scare hunters off the property—and I can assure you he's very effective at it! When hunting season opens, the place is crawling with poachers, and Uncle Albert doesn't like it at all."

Janine nodded, not willing to trust her voice at the moment. Sitting there beside Frederick on the damp chilly sand, watching the swans gliding by in the late-afternoon sunlight, she felt almost as she'd felt that day when the storm had driven her inside the cave—as if she'd been transported to a world that had nothing to do with reality.

"How did your first week go?" Frederick asked, startling her back to the present. As he spoke he reached over and put his arm around her shoulders.

"Oh, it was fine," she said distractedly.

"Did Karla bother you?"

She looked at him, at his warm gray eyes and his curly blond hair glinting in the dying rays of the sun, and suddenly she began to feel much better, as if somehow his mere presence reassured her.

"Nothing I couldn't handle," she said, returning his affectionate smile. "But she certainly is one of the most unpleasant people I've ever met!"

Frederick was silent for a few moments. He sat

staring out over the lake, taking in the beauty of the sunset reflected on the smooth water, and the swans with their long arched necks moving by.

"This has always been one of my favorite places," he said softly. "We used to play here when we were children—Karla and I, and André and Jacques. . . ."

Janine shuddered involuntarily, not sure what had made her do so.

"Are you cold?" Frederick asked.

Before she could answer Frederick had whipped off his corduroy jacket and placed it over her shoulders. Again she was reminded of that stormy day in the cave, and the way the stranger had placed his jacket over her shoulders because she was cold.

"Let's go back now," she said, starting to rise.

"Janine, what's the matter?" Frederick asked, his voice full of concern. "Are you sure Karla didn't upset you?"

"No, really. . . I just. . .I just want to take a nap before dinner—that's all. Really."

He rose and put his arm around her. "Janine— you're trembling!" he exclaimed. "What's wrong?"

"It's nothing, Frederick, really. Please. . .let's just go back to the castle."

It was already dusk as they made their way along the path. Frederick kept his arm securely around her, and she liked the strength and warmth he offered her.

"I really did miss you," he whispered in her ear.

She stopped abruptly and smiled up at him. "You know, I really missed you, too!" She realized then that she'd missed him more than she'd been aware of.

"How long can you stay?" she asked as they continued their walk.

"I'm not sure. A few days, anyway, I think. But I'd like to show you around the grounds—there's lots you haven't seen yet. Maybe tomorrow we can pack a picnic lunch and I'll take you to—"

"But I have work to do!" Janine interrupted, laughing. "Unless your uncle will give me time off for good behavior!"

"Your sense of humor delights me," Frederick said, and his voice was much deeper now than she'd ever heard it before. "And so do your blue eyes and your bronze-colored hair—"

Unsure how to react to such compliments Janine blushed and broke away from him to run up the path.

"Wait!" he called after her. "I want us to arrive together. André—that's Karla's husband—just got back and I want you to meet him!"

Janine stopped dead in her tracks, and again that cold, uncomfortable tingle began to creep up her spine.

She felt like she was in a trance as she climbed the stone steps to the front door and walked into the vast dim entrance hall, with Frederick close behind her.

She heard voices coming from the drawing room, and instinctively put her hands up to tidy the wisps of hair that had escaped the hold of the barrette.

"Don't touch a single strand!" Frederick admonished, "You look absolutely beautiful just the way you are!"

She smiled, then caught her breath as she heard what seemed like a familiar voice. . . .

Fighting a rising panic she managed to appear calm as she followed Frederick into the drawing room.

The count was standing in front of the enormous marble fireplace. Karla stood beside him, looking smashing in a white cocktail dress that fit tightly, her raven-black hair pulled back into an intricately braided bun. Facing her was a tall man with dark wavy hair, and from the back he looked very impressive in a charcoal-gray pin-striped suit.

"André!" Frederick called as he and Janine advanced into the room, hand in hand. "I want you to meet someone!"

The man turned around slowly, but Janine knew who it was even before she saw his face. It was the man who'd held her that night in the cave. . . .

For what seemed an eternity but was in reality only a few seconds, they stared at each other in silence.

He seemed composed, but she thought he looked a little paler than she remembered. There was nothing about his expression to indicate that he recognized her.

The count stepped forward and said, "André, this is Miss Janine Aubry. She's taking care of that genealogical research I've been so interested in."

Then, turning to Janine, he added, "Miss Aubry, I'm proud to present my son-in-law, André Gerard."

"It's a great pleasure to meet you, Miss Aubry," André said, extending his hand.

Don't you even remember me, Janine longed to ask him, but the look on his face warned her not to.

"How do you do," she said, allowing him to clasp her hand.

As their hands touched, she felt the cold metal of his wedding ring. But he hadn't worn a ring when they'd first met. . . .

And then she thought: of course married men away on business trips...other women.... How incredibly naive she'd been!

Anger and pain seared through her, and she averted her face to hide the awful expression she knew she wore.

"Janine and I were just down at the lake watching the swans," Frederick was saying.

"I'm glad you finally decided to get out and see something of the countryside," the count remarked pleasantly. "It's a crime for a young girl like you to stay locked away in the library day after day without a break."

As he finished speaking the drawing-room door opened and Hans walked in, clad as usual in his black butler's tuxedo, his hawklike face as grim as ever.

"Well, Uncle Albert, I'm certainly glad to hear you say so," Frederick said in reply to the count's comment. "Especially since Janine and I had planned to take a little excursion into the woods tomorrow, and maybe take along a picnic lunch." He had his back to the door and hadn't seen Hans enter.

The count smiled and nodded his approval, then turned toward Hans with a quizzical look.

The butler bowed formally and announced, "Dinner will be served in half an hour, sir."

"Thank you, Hans," the count said.

When Hans had left the room the count turned back to Janine. "A picnic sounds like a wonderful idea. In fact, since tomorrow is Sunday I insist that you take the whole day. If I find you in the library I shall be extremely displeased!" he teased, his pale blue eyes twinkling with merriment.

Janine mumbled something indistinct; she couldn't possibly trust her voice now.

She sensed André smiling at her, his eyes just as intensely green as ever, and again she averted her face. She couldn't bear the feelings he was stirring up within her.

"Perhaps you'd like to change before dinner?" the count inquired politely, taking in the faded old blue jeans and sweater Janine was wearing.

She nodded, and then Frederick took her hand and began to lead her back out to the hall. Her knees were trembling so violently that she was certain she couldn't have walked without his assistance.

Alone in her room, Janine sat on the bed staring out the window at the night sky. Her feelings were so confused and so powerful that she couldn't think clearly.

Finally after all the long weeks of yearning and longing, and dreaming, she'd found him . . . only to discover the reason for his mysterious disappearance.

His wife. . . .

Janine shuddered. How could he have married her? How could he have chosen Karla? Of course, there was no denying she was exceptionally beautiful, but still . . . .

And again Janine felt that rage flare. Only this time it was directed inward, at herself. She couldn't blame him. It was her own fault that she'd fallen for him. Silently she cursed herself for her naiveté, her girlish romanticism, her utter stupidity!

But how was she going to deal with the situation?

She hadn't been working for the count long enough to have earned enough money to leave and find her-

self a new job. Nor could she return to the old one—
she'd resigned her position with the agency and had
given up her apartment.

The frustration she began to feel was unbearable.

Suddenly she thought of Frederick, of his warm
smile and twinkly eyes. Well, if nothing else, she at
least had one comforting reassuring friendship. . . .

Chapter 9

During dinner Janine had an opportunity to observe André and Karla together. They were a strikingly handsome couple, and he seemed to be the model husband. He was attentive and courteous, and Karla seemed to hang on his every word. Drunk though she obviously was, there was no evidence tonight of her usual hostility. Her eyes were glazed over, yet they lacked that wild gleam that often made her look so crazy.

Janine was wondering if André really loved her— or, if he didn't now, if he had when they'd first been married. Then she asked herself what difference it made anyway. The fact that he was a married man was all that mattered; even if his marriage wasn't a happy one Janine still couldn't pursue the relationship with him that she knew she wanted.

Frederick sat next to her at dinner and lavished her with endless compliments, but she seemed not to hear him. Finally in exasperation he said to her, "Janine, you're not even listening to me!" His tone conveyed both anger and hurt.

"But of course I am," she replied calmly.

Then, realizing that he was right, she felt guilty, and covered his hand with hers. "I'm sorry, Frederick. I was just thinking about something. Now what were you saying?"

"I was saying that instead of going to the lake for our picnic tomorrow, I thought it'd be nice to hike to a little clearing in the woods about half a mile beyond the lake. We used to have our picnics there when we were children."

"That sounds wonderful," Janine murmured, wishing that dinner would end and she could escape to the privacy of her room. She couldn't bear the pain of watching André and Karla together.

Hans was standing behind her, his asthmatic breathing rattling in her ears.

"Coffee, Miss?" he asked in his deep sonorous voice.

Janine shook her head no. Ever since he'd poured the scalding coffee into her lap that first day, she'd refused to take even a single cup.

"Anyway," Frederick went on, "it's a beautiful spot. It's off the same path that leads to the lake."

As Hans poured coffee into Frederick's cup, he looked up at the butler and said, "Hans, please ask the chef to pack us a picnic lunch tomorrow morning."

"At what time will you be leaving, sir?" Hans asked.

Frederick looked at Janine as if expecting her to

name the time, but apparently she was lost in her thoughts again.

"Oh, ten or ten-thirty, I guess," he said, and Hans nodded then went around the table pouring coffee for the others.

"Remember that hunting season opens in a few days," the count said to his nephew. "Ernst will probably be around the grounds tomorrow setting traps and the like. So watch your step!"

Frederick said that of course he would be careful, and then they went on to talk of other things.

When dinner was over they adjourned to the small salon where Janine and Frederick had sat listening to Beethoven the first night she'd spent at the castle. At the count's request—and André's urging—Karla agreed to play the harp for them, and Janine was surprised at the skill with which she played. Karla had struck her as being anything but sensitive, but the way she strummed the harp made her acutely aware how wrong she'd been.

Janine settled herself on the satin-upholstered sofa and leaned back into the cushions, enjoying the soft melodic strains of the music. When Frederick seated himself at the piano and began to accompany Karla, the effect was quite beautiful.

Janine was just beginning to relax, allowing the horrible thoughts that had been racing around in her head to begin to quiet down, when André joined her on the sofa and lighted a cigarette.

"You don't mind?" he asked, referring to the cigarette.

The anger that she'd just succeeded in repressing suddenly rose again.

"Don't tell me you've forgotten already!" she said sharply. "I like the smell of cigarettes!"

André ignored her, asking quietly, "How did you manage to find me?"

"Don't flatter yourself. I wasn't looking for you. I placed an ad in some newspapers, looking for free-lance work as a researcher, and the count responded to my ad. That's all there was to it. Anyway, you certainly went to great efforts to ensure that I wouldn't find you. Meeting you here, now, is merely a coincidence—a very bizarre coincidence, and, I might add, an uncomfortable one."

"Under the circumstances, it seemed better that way," he said.

Karla was still playing, but her eyes were riveted to the sofa where he and Janine sat.

Janine looked into his face, trying to read his expression. What was he feeling? She couldn't say. But somehow he looked older now than he had that day in the cave. There were wrinkles around his eyes that hadn't been there—or perhaps she just hadn't noticed them. The cleft in his chin looked even deeper.

Unconsciously she shook her head as if to clear away all the warm happy memories that were beginning to haunt her once again.

"You don't understand," he said softly. "And I can't explain it. . . ."

"What's there to understand?" Janine said dully.

Try as she might she couldn't keep the hurt from sounding in her voice. "You weren't wearing a wedding ring. . . ."

"At the time, I. . . ." He hesitated. "I wasn't wearing a ring—but I still wasn't free, either."

Janine said nothing. She couldn't bring herself to look at him. How was it possible to feel such love and such pain at the same time, she wondered. For she knew now without any doubt that she loved him....

"I'm not going to try to justify my actions," André said simply. "It wouldn't be of any use. But please believe that I never meant to deceive or hurt you."

Janine knew that this was true. He hadn't lied to her during their time together in the cave. He hadn't made any promises, nor had he made any avowals of love for her. He had kissed her, and in her foolish romanticism she'd read all sorts of meanings into that. She had allowed his warmly supportive words to mean much more to her than he had intended.

Apparently he sensed what she was thinking, and she was startled when he said, "I wasn't playing games with you or trying to trick you, Janine. It was...well, let's say it was just a moment of weakness on my part. For a few moments I allowed myself to forget my obligations."

Despite the frantic beating of her heart, Janine managed to maintain a calm smiling expression. They were talking softly, hoping not to draw the attention of the others in the room, but obviously Karla was not about to take her eyes off the two of them.

As André caught the menacing look on his wife's face, he said to Janine in an urgent tone, "You can't stay here. You've got to leave as soon as possible."

"Why?" Janine asked.

"Because...because under the circumstances it's quite impossible for you to stay here!"

"That doesn't answer my question, André. Why should I leave?"

He looked at her with exasperation.

"Just think about it for a minute, will you? No possible good can come from you prolonging your stay at Weisdorf. The longer you stay, the harder it will be for both of us. Surely you can understand that?"

Janine knew that, despite her financial position, the wisest thing for her to do at this point would be to leave. She could invent some excuse to explain why she suddenly had to quit her research. But she couldn't bring herself to do that. It was partly that she was just now getting to the part of the work that she found most fascinating and she wanted to see it through to the end. But even more, she wanted to stay near André now that she'd found him.

"I won't leave until I've completed my work," she said, deliberately keeping her voice flat and emotionless. "I work for the count and I take my orders from him. If and when he dismisses me I'll go. Until then I have no intention of doing so."

She felt another stab of pain, then added, "And I have no intention of leaving simply because it would be more convenient for you not to have me here!"

At this point Emma entered the salon, carrying a tray with a crystal decanter full of brandy and five brandy snifters.

Taking in the sight of André and Janine deep in private conversation on the sofa, she shot them a look full of hatred, then proceeded farther into the room and set the tray on a side table near the harp. Karla looked up and smiled at her, and for a few seconds they exchanged wordless glances that seemed full of meaning. Then Emma nodded briskly, as if Karla had actually said something to her, and turned and strode out of the room with a last malevolent look at Janine as she passed the sofa.

The count crossed the room to the side table and began to pour out brandies for everyone as André turned to whisper to Janine. "To stay here is insane! You've got to leave! Don't you see—if you stay it's going to be unbearable for us both."

"Why, not at all!" Janine replied with mock bravado. "There's no problem. You're married—I accept that. These things happen sometimes. We'll just forget what happened, that's all. And, come to think of it, there's really nothing to forget."

The music came to an end and the count stood in front of them, holding two brandy snifters.

"A nightcap," he said, handing them each a glass.

Janine murmured a thank-you and then turned away from André as Frederick rose from the piano and came over to them.

"So you two are getting acquainted!" he said, beaming with obvious pleasure.

"Yes, we are," Janine replied calmly.

"Janine was just telling me about the time she spent in Paris," André remarked conversationally.

"Well, with all the time you've been spending there lately, setting up that second Mercedes dealership, I guess the two of you have a lot in common," Frederick said.

"Yes, as a matter of fact," André replied.

Janine looked from André to Frederick and back again to André. She couldn't believe the banality of this conversation, but in a way it was a relief after the heated words she'd just had with André.

But then Karla appeared at Frederick's side. In one hand she held a long gold-enameled cigarette holder; in the other was a snifter of brandy.

"You two certainly seem to be hitting it off well," she said in an irritated voice.

"We were just discussing life in Paris," André said easily; but Janine didn't miss the warning glance he shot at his wife.

"I'll bet!" Karla retorted. "From the expressions on your faces, it must have been a most absorbing topic!"

Her tone was becoming increasingly aggressive, and the count came rushing over, a worried look on his face.

André, apparently sensing that there was an unpleasant scene in the making, rose from the sofa and gently pried the brandy snifter from Karla's hand.

"You must be tired, Karla," he said firmly but softly. "Come on, I'll go upstairs with you."

Then he turned to Janine and said a very cool good-night.

His arm around Karla's waist, he led her out of the room.

The count, apparently relieved that an unpleasant scene had been avoided, settled himself in a wing chair and began to read a newspaper.

Janine was about to excuse herself and go on up to bed when Frederick suddenly grabbed her hand and pulled her over to the stereo, where he put on a beautiful Straus waltz.

She hadn't really wanted to dance, but his graceful, fluid movements were easy to follow, and the
strength of his arms around her was comforting.

"You dance marvelously," he whispered into her
ear. "But then, everything about you is marvelous!"

Chapter 10

"You're not seriously planning to wear *that*, are you?" Frederick laughed with amazement. "We're going for a hike—not a stroll down the Champs-Elysées!"

Janine accepted his blunt hint, and turned around to begin the long climb back up the stone staircase. Well, perhaps he was right—low-slung pumps and a light cotton dress might not be appropriate clothing for a hike.

She was reminded of another day, not too long ago, when her clothing had been inappropriate for a walk along a path that wound upward through boulders and thorny bushes.. . .

No, she absolutely would not think about it! Not today, at any rate. Today she would forget everything except the beauty of the countryside and the pleasure of Frederick's company.

Having changed into a pair of snug-fitting blue corduroy dungarees and a white sweater, and exchanging her pumps for sturdy shoes, she hurried back down to the entrance hall where Frederick was waiting for her.

They set off hand in hand across the lawn, Frederick carrying the wicker picnic basket under one arm.

After crossing the rose garden he led her onto the same path that she'd taken yesterday to get to the lake. But soon he steered her off of it and onto another one that was much narrower and obviously not used very often.

"I thought you said it was off the path that goes to the lake," she remarked.

"It is, but the view from this path is much nicer. Anyway, both paths wind up meeting at the same little clearing."

They rounded a bend and were greeted with a magnificent sight—a view of deep crevices and ravines with shining streams winding through them—and once again Janine marveled at the diversity of the countryside, now gentle and peaceful, now wild and unrestrained. She felt she could never tire of the incredibly blue sky, the towering mountain peaks and black pine forests, the lush green pastures, and the cascading waterfalls that shone like a million fragments of mirror-glass in the sun.

"It's breathtaking," she murmured as she stood there drinking in the beauty of it.

"So are you," Frederick said softly, and gave her hand a little squeeze.

Janine smiled at him and they continued along the path. Squirrels were chattering noisily as they leaped from branch to branch overhead, their springtime mating sounds filling the air.

Suddenly there was a rustling in the bushes at the side of the path, and within seconds Ernst and his snarling German shepherd appeared.

"Good morning!" Frederick said. And to the dog, who was growling and sniffing around his ankles, "Take it easy, Wolf. That's a good boy. Easy now."

He reached down and patted the dog's head. Instantly the dog stopped snarling and began to wag his tail in friendly fashion.

Janine sidled closer to Frederick; she didn't like the dog at all, and the double-barreled shotgun that Ernst carried over his shoulder made her very uneasy.

"Setting your traps against this season's poachers?" he asked the gamekeeper.

Ernst grunted in reply.

"Well, see you around!" Frederick said cheerfully, and he and Janine continued on their way.

The path began to slope downward now, and as the ground was covered with damp rotting leaves, Janine had a little difficulty keeping her footing. Frederick stopped to pick up a piece of a branch that was lying at the side of the path, and handed it to her to use as a walking stick.

As they rounded another bend, Frederick stopped and said, "At last!"

Janine was enthralled. The tiny clearing was almost perfectly circular, and the perimeter of it was lined with low flat stones. At the center of the clearing was another much smaller circle of stones, which Janine assumed had been used for building fires. Enormous pines towered around them, making a sort of canopy over the clearing, and their thick, dark green branches shut out much of the sunlight. However, it was anything but gloomy, for there were spots where the sunshine filtered through and dappled the ground with patches of yellow and gold.

"I'm going to spread out the tablecloth over there," Frederick said, pointing toward the little circle of stones. "Why don't you clear away some of the wet leaves while I start unpacking the basket."

Janine walked on ahead of him, using the walking stick he'd given her to push away the wet rotting vegetation.

Suddenly there was a loud metallic *clank* and Janine screamed, dropping the stick as she jumped back.

"What is it?" Frederick shouted, running up to her.

Janine just stood there trembling, pointing at the ground.

The stick lay there in front of her, one end of it neatly severed. An old rusted iron trap with menacing-looking serrated jaws lay beside it; the severed end of the stick was clamped tight in the trap.

"That's just one of the traps that Ernst puts out every year," Frederick soothed.

Janine shuddered as she looked at the sharklike teeth of the trap, imagining the pain it would cause to an animal who happened to set its paw down on it.

"What kind of animal is it intended for?" she asked. "It looks like an old-fashioned bear trap."

"That's exactly what it is. But is isn't meant to catch animals—it's for the poachers."

"You mean the count has Ernst put out traps like that for hunters? For human beings?" Janine shuddered again. "Why, that thing would slice a man's foot right off!"

"No it wouldn't," Frederick assured her. "When Ernst first came up with the idea of setting out the traps, Uncle Albert insisted that he modify them so that they'd cause some pain but wouldn't do any real damage. So Ernst loosened the springs that control the tension of the jaw." He set down the picnic basket and picked up the trap. "See?" He pulled the serrated jaws wide apart to demonstrate.

"All the same," Janine said, still feeling shaken, "it'd be excrutiating, I'm sure." She realized that she could very easily have caught her foot in the trap.

"Oh, come on, it's nothing to get upset about," Frederick said as he put his arms around her. "Anyway, hunters always wear heavy boots, so the worst thing they'd get is a big bruise."

She was still trembling, and he hugged her close against him. Then, before she knew what was happening, Frederick's lips found hers.

It was a brief gentle kiss, and although it didn't arouse in Janine anything approaching the rapture of André's kisses, it did give her a warm happy feeling.

Frederick released her and began spreading the cloth and laying out plates. Janine settled herself comfortably on the ground, folding her legs Indian-fashion in front of her.

Frederick poured out two glasses of white wine and handed one to her. "To us!" he announced, beaming with pleasure.

She smiled in reply, and touched her glass to his.

The food was delicious, as she'd come to expect by now. The count's French chef had packed the perfect picnic—cold chicken, three different kinds of cheese, a loaf of French bread, and chilled white wine.

"How's your research work coming along?" Frederick asked as she nibbled at a chicken wing. "Found any skeletons in the family closet?"

"Not yet," Janine answered happily. "But soon, maybe. I've finished cataloging all the old land deeds and bank accounts and things like that. Next week I'm going to start on the personal letters." She paused. "If there's any connection between the von Erlichs and Ludwig the Second, I think I'll find it in those letters."

"You really do enjoy your work, don't you?" Frederick asked.

Janine nodded, and he went on, "It must be nice to make your living doing something that really interests you. I'm envious."

Janine looked at him in surprise. "Don't you like being a lawyer?"

"No, not really. Actually, it's a bore. Maybe by the time I've become a senior partner in the firm it'll change, but for now all I do is handle divorce proceedings—not only dull, but depressing, too. People get married, thinking they're going to spend their lives together—and then they end up tearing each other apart in the divorce courts." He shook his head sadly.

"Well, your uncle certainly seems proud of your being a lawyer," she commented.

"I'm glad he is. I think he was afraid I'd turn out like Jacques—André's younger brother. Jacques was a happy-go-lucky boy, full of fun and adventure, and without a single ambition in life, short of marrying Karla."

Janine looked at him in astonishment. "Karla?" she

repeated. "You mean Jacques and Karla were engaged before he was killed?"

Seeing Frederick's look of surprise, she quickly added, "The count told me about it. . . ."

"Exactly what did he tell you?" Frederick asked, and Janine thought for a second that there was a strange note in his voice—almost one of suspicion.

"Just that he was killed in an automobile accident in Switzerland, that's all," she answered. "Why?"

"Nothing, really." He paused for a few moments before he went on. "Well, I don't think Jacques and Karla were actually engaged, but they did spend a lot of time together right before he was killed. Jacques had always been madly in love with her."

"And she with him?" Janine asked, full of curiosity.

Frederick shook his head. "Not her! She had her sights set on André all along."

Janine wasn't sure what to make of this, but she wanted to find out a great deal more.

In as casual and disinterested a voice as she could, she ventured, "It's really none of my business, but it struck me last night that André and Karla seem . . . oh, I'm not sure how to put it. I guess what I'm trying to say is that they don't seem suited to each other. Don't you think so?"

"André's a wonderful man—much too good for her!" Frederick said, sounding angry.

Then, in a completely different tone of voice, he added, "Let's not waste our time talking about them. We're here in this beautiful place, alone together, and I don't want anything to spoil it."

Janine struggled to mask her disappointment.

There was nothing she'd like more at the moment than to go on delving into the mystery of André and his wife. But Frederick's tone made it clear that he wasn't going to continue.

There was a silence for a few moments, during which Frederick refilled their wineglasses, then lay back and looked at Janine's face.

"You're very beautiful, Janine," he said softly. "I thought about you all week while I was in Munich. And last night when we danced, I wanted to go on holding you in my arms. . . ."

Blushing and feeling very awkward, Janine looked away from him. "If you keep saying things like that, I'm going to become insufferably conceited!" she said, hoping to lighten what she sensed was about to become a very emotional conversation.

"You have every right to be conceited," Frederick persisted, his voice very deep and husky now. "Janine, I'm falling in love with you."

She looked at him in astonishment, not sure what to say.

"I know we haven't known each other very long," he went on, "but I know what I feel, Janine. What I don't know is how *you* feel."

Janine looked at him silently, trying to find the right words to express her feelings. Love? She'd never even considered it where Frederick was concerned.

"I. . .I'm very fond of you, Frederick," she said in a near whisper. "And since I first came to the castle I've come to rely on your friendship and your support. But I don't think. . .well, I haven't known you very long, and I think that for two people to be genuinely in love, they have to know each other quite well."

As she spoke she knew she was lying; she'd known Frederick much longer than she'd known André, yet she didn't doubt for one second that what she felt for André was love.

Frederick shook his head sadly, but the twinkle in his eyes was still there.

"I guess I expected you to say something like that. I know it sounds crazy—'love at first sight'—but I think that's what happened to me.... All I'm asking, Janine, is if you think there's a chance for us...after you've had a chance to get to know me better."

"I don't know, Frederick. Honestly. Maybe there's a chance—maybe not. How *could* I know?"

"I'm not going to make all sorts of promises and declarations, because I don't want to frighten you away or make you feel overwhelmed. But, Janine, I love you with all my heart, and I'll wait as long as it takes for you to love me back."

He reached out and took her hand.

"I'll wait forever, if you want me to."

He turned her hand over and pressed his lips against her palm, then against the soft underside of her wrist.

"All I need is a little encouragement from you... some sign that you think there's a chance for us to be together."

His eyes looked deeply into hers. "Can you give me that, Janine?"

She ached all over with the knowledge that her love for André was futile and that to go on loving him would mean nothing but pain for the rest of her life. And now here was this warm wonderful man, ready to love and cherish her.... But what could she give him? Would it be fair to him to let him love her when she loved someone else?

"I don't know what to say, Frederick. This is so sudden.... I need time to think."

As she spoke she turned her face toward him—and there was that disarming smile of his, the one she could never help but return. And as her answering smile spread across her face, she realized that she *did* love him. But it was the kind of love she would have felt for a brother, if she'd had one; it wasn't anything like the love she felt for André.

Well, she thought, it was possible that her affection for Frederick could change....

"I'll try, Frederick," she said softly.

"No!" he said fiercely, dropping her hand. "I don't want you to 'try' anything! You can't make efforts to love someone—either you love that person or you don't. 'Trying' doesn't even enter into it."

"You're right," she said, feeling ashamed of herself. "I'm sorry I said that. I guess what I mean is this—I'll keep my heart and my mind open to you. If I find myself falling in love with you...." She smiled shyly, not sure what words to use to finish the sentence.

"Oh, Janine, I love you so much!" he cried, and pulled her into his arms. "As long as you'll keep yourself open to the possibility...that's all I can ask—all I *will* ask. But, my darling, I want you to know that I mean to marry you."

He kissed her, softly at first, then with greater insistence. She returned the kiss, though with somewhat less passion, then buried her face against his shoulder.

She was trying to blot out the memory of André's

kisses and the warm wonderful sensations he'd aroused in her. And yet, at the same time, she was also trying to evoke those same sensations now with Frederick, because she genuinely cared for him. She wanted to love him as he loved her and as she loved André.

His lips pressing softly against her forehead, he said in a deep whisper, "I won't ask you to commit yourself to marriage right away. Just think about it. Take all the time you need. I'll wait, Janine."

Chapter 11

"Leave...while you can...while there's still time...
leave...leave...*now!*"

Janine looked up into the faces that hovered over
her as she lay helpless on the ground.

Emma, Hans and Ernst, Hans's brother—chanting
at her, warning her to leave the castle before....

With a gasp, Janine sat bolt upright in her bed. Her
whole body was covered with a cold sweat, her
hands were trembling uncontrollably, and her bed-
sheets were a twisted crumpled mess.

She was filled with an indefinable terror.

And then she slumped back against the pillows and
sighed heavily. A dream—that was all. Just a nightmare.

She looked over to the windows judging the time
by the light. It was about seven o'clock, and she
thought she heard the distant hum of Frederick's car
driving down the steep twisting mountain road, en
route to his job in Munich.

She shook her head, stretched her slender arms high over her head, yawned, considered getting up, then decided at the last minute to try to go back to sleep.

"Leave now...while you still can...now, now, *now!*"

This time their faces were distorted, grotesque, like evil masks. Hans held a pot of scalding hot coffee over her face, while Ernst grinned malevolently as he snapped the iron jaws of the bear trap over her foot.

"Get out now...while you can...while you can...while you can," they chanted.

Janine reassured herself again that it was only a nightmare and fell into a light uneasy sleep.

Later as she washed and dressed, the feeling of the horrid dream remained with her, gnawing painfully in the pit of her stomach.

Looking into the mirror as she brushed her teeth, she had a flashback of the dream—there stood Hans, about to scald her face with hot coffee, and Ernst, clamping the trap onto her foot.

Now just cut it out, she told herself sternly.

But she'd never been able to shake the feeling that Hans had deliberately poured the coffee into her lap that first day; and now came the feeling—equally strong—that Ernst had set that trap in the clearing particularly for her.

No, she decided, she was just being paranoid. Why would Ernst do such a thing? And besides, how could he have known that she and Frederick would go to that particular spot in the woods?

Then came the sickening memory...Hans hovering behind Frederick at dinner the other night while he was telling Janine where he was planning to take her for the picnic....

The nightmare continued to haunt her throughout the morning, despite her efforts to concentrate fully on her work in the library. Try as she might she couldn't rid herself of what was now almost a certainty—Hans and Ernst had done those things purposely. But why? That was the part she couldn't grasp.

Perhaps it all came back to Karla: Karla obviously didn't want her at the castle; therefore Emma didn't want her there either. And hadn't Frederick told her that Hans was kept tightly under Emma's thumb? If Emma had told her husband and his brother to do whatever they could to make her want to leave....

Did that make sense, she wondered. It would be a relief when Frederick returned. There were many questions that he could answer for her, and she felt that she needed his support now more than ever.

Frederick....

She tried not to think about his declaration of love and his wish to marry her. He'd said he wouldn't rush her but would give her all the time she wanted, to think, to come to a decision, so she didn't feel any pressing need to do anything about the situation right now.

Right now, she reminded herself, she had a job to do. With fresh determination, she picked up a pile of old birth certificates and began to arrange them chronologically, giving scant attention to the names they bore.

When Hilda knocked on the library door and called in to her that luncheon would be served in half an hour, Janine gave up on the paperwork. She hadn't really been able to get involved in it this morning, so she decided to stop trying and go up to her room to wash before lunch. The documents she'd been working on were old and dusty, and after a few hours of handling them her hands were badly in need of washing.

She made her way quickly through the maze of stone corridors that wound back to the large dim entrance hall. Suddenly she found herself face to face with André at the foot of the stairs.

He had just come out through one of the mirror-covered doors, and as he caught sight of her, he smiled, then the smile turned into almost a grimace. He just stood there, very still, waiting as she approached.

Her mind was racing frantically as she walked toward him, trying to summon as much emotional strength as she could.

"Good morning," she said curtly when she was within a few feet of where he stood.

Then as she tried to continue on past him and go upstairs, he grabbed her by the arm.

"Janine," he said, his voice like steel, "I must insist that you leave Weisdorf. Immediately."

She glared at him with a mixture of astonishment and fury.

"I'm a real embarrassment to you, aren't I?" she demanded.

André shook his head wearily. "What do you hope to gain by staying here?" he asked.

His hand was still wrapped tightly around her arm, and she shook herself free of it before she answered in a cold reasonable voice. "I work here. I'm being paid to do a job—a job that interests me! And after all, isn't that what you yourself encouraged me to do— find a job I really cared about and then stick with it? No," she said calmly, "there's no reason why I should leave. I've done nothing wrong. What happened between us in the first place wasn't my fault—it was yours, André."

"Good God, don't you think I know that! And I'm not accusing you of anything. We shared something very special and wonderful that night, but now—" He broke off, then continued, "Look, I'm prepared to pay whatever price I must for the time we spent together, but you . . .*please*, Janine, tell the count that you have to leave—tell him that you're sick, or that someone in Paris sent for you—tell him anything! If you need money, I'll be happy—"

"You'd do anything at all to avoid a confrontation with your wife, wouldn't you?" Janine said softly.

"Leave my wife out of this," André said, his tone oddly sad when Janine had expected it to be full of anger.

Then all her pent-up rage came pouring out before she could stop it.

"Why should I leave her out of it? Do you think I'm blind as well as stupid? It's quite clear that she's at the bottom of all this—that it's to make her happy that you're trying to send me away! But it isn't going to work, André!" Her blue eyes were flashing with anger and her voice was full of bitterness.

"You're wrong, Janine." His voice was soft now, and heavy with sadness. "You haven't any idea how wrong you are. But I can't explain it to you . . .not now, anyway. And you're so young—things like duty and honor probably don't even make sense to you."

She looked at him, puzzled by what he'd just said, not sure what he meant or how she should react.

Impulsively he reached out and took her hand. "Please, Janine," he said, his intense green eyes probing hers, "try to understand." With that he raised her hand to his lips and tenderly kissed her palm. "Please....you've got to help me. I can't stand the temptation of having you so near," he whispered, his lips still lingering against her hand. "Please don't make it any harder for me than it is already."

The dim light from the high narrow windows created shadows across his face, making his features appear harsh and deeply etched. But for Janine he was once again the handsome wonderful stranger in whose arms she'd slept that stormy night in the cave. She felt herself beginning to weaken, as if her insides were melting. His lips still lingered caressingly against the palm of her hand, sending electric sensations up her arm and raising goosebumps on her flesh.

Suddenly all the warm sensations he'd aroused in her turned to ice.

"I don't believe you! All you can think about is the security and happiness of your marriage, now that you're home. But I'm here to do a job—and that's all."

"No, Janine!" He reached for her hand again, but she whipped it around behind her. "It has nothing to do with the happiness of my marriage, as you put it. I have other reasons for feeling the way I do. Very serious reasons."

She looked up at him hesitantly, desperately wanting to believe him.

"All right, André. Tell me what those reasons are, and I'll try to understand." She was hoping against hope that he would tell her something that would ease the awful ache she felt inside.

"I can't do that," he said slowly. "At least, not now. But I beg of you—trust me. Believe me when I say it's not wise for you to stay here!"

One of the mirror-covered doors suddenly opened and Emma stepped into the hall. She glared at them for a moment, taking in the way they were standing so closely together. Then she mumbled something under her breath as she passed them and began to climb the stairs.

André and Janine exchanged one last wordless look, then went their separate ways.

ANDRE LEFT EARLY the following morning. Janine heard him start the engine of his Mercedes, and she rushed to her bedroom window, parted the curtains and looked down. He chose that moment to look up, and she stepped back quickly, praying that he hadn't seen her. She wanted him to believe that his leaving was a matter of complete indifference to her. In fact she wanted to believe that herself, but she knew it was far from the truth.

Later, she gulped down her breakfast, pausing just long enough to say a few polite words to the count, then escaped to the library, which was fast becoming her own private sanctum.

Today, she promised herself as she sat down at the long table, she would concentrate hard on her work.

She'd use it to keep her mind off all the things that she didn't want to think about or deal with right now.

Before her lay the stack of old birth certificates that she'd started working on yesterday, putting them into chronological order. Resolutely she pulled the stack toward her.

Yes, she thought, it would be good to get back into her work, to feel the excitement of uncovering the past, trying to unravel whatever secrets lay hidden among the count's ancestors. . . .

After an hour she pushed the stack of papers away from her. It was no use. Her mind simply wouldn't focus on anything.

How could everything have gone so wrong so quickly, she wondered. A few weeks ago she'd been filled with strength, confidence, hope, excitement about creating a new life for herself . . . and now she was plagued by doubts and confusion about everything. Added to that was the fact that the work that she'd found so absorbing now seemed dull and lifeless. She couldn't concentrate on it at all.

She swiveled her chair around and leaned back to gaze up at the high-vaulted ceiling, trying to shut off her painful thoughts and feelings.

Taking a deep breath to steady her shaky nerves, she closed her eyes, hoping she might doze off for a little while and forget about everything.

A sharp loud knock on the library door startled her.

She was about to call out, "Come in!" but she didn't get a chance. The door opened and in strode Emma, hands firmly planted against her wide hips.

"Frau Karla wishes to see you immediately!" she announced.

"Really?" Janine said wearily, feeling that even the effort of speaking was more than she could handle. "What does she want?"

"You'll find that out soon enough!" Emma snapped.

Janine felt like telling her that she wasn't in Karla's employ and had no intention of taking orders from her, but it seemed like too great an effort to argue. Besides, she couldn't help feeling a little bit curious as to what Karla wanted to see her about. With Karla there was never any way of predicting anything.

"All right," Janine said quietly.

Chapter 12

Emma led her through a part of the castle that she hadn't seen before, but it was much the same—mazes of stone corridors that felt damp and chilly. Finally they came to a narrow twisting staircase and began to climb. When they reached the third-floor landing, Emma pulled a key on a long chain out of her pocket and proceeded down a long dimly lighted corridor.

"Frau Karla likes her privacy," she remarked as she halted before a heavy wooden door and inserted the key into an ancient-looking iron lock. She twisted the key, then pushed the door open. "Well, go in!" she ordered.

Janine glanced at her uncertainly, then proceeded ahead of her into the room.

There was no way Janine could have anticipated the spectacle that greeted her eyes.

Here, it could have been night. Heavy brocade curtains covered all the walls from floor to ceiling, so that if there were any windows in the room they were completely hidden. The room was lighted by candles—seemingly hundreds of them—in enormous silver candelabras. It was a warm day, yet there was a roaring blaze in the marble-hearthed fireplace.

The heavy baroque furniture that filled the other rooms in the castle was here, too, but in even greater abundance. The room was so crowded with furniture that it was hard for Janine to see a clear pathway across to where Karla was half lying, half sitting, on a satin chaise longue.

She was wearing turquoise silk lounging pajamas, and, as usual, her face was thickly covered with makeup. In one hand was a cigarette smoldering in a long gold holder; in the other hand was a glass of whiskey. There was a low massive-looking wooden table in front of the chaise, and on it stood a half-empty bottle of Scotch. That wild crazy-looking gleam was back in her eyes again, and Janine felt distinctly uncomfortable as she realized that Karla was staring directly at her but apparently didn't see her. In fact she seemed completely unaware that Janine had even entered.

There were magazines and newspapers strewn all over the carpet around the chaise, and from an old stereo in the far corner of the room came the soft muted strains of a Bach composition.

The atmosphere in the room was unbearable. It was unbelievably hot and stuffy, and the combined odors of stale cigarette smoke and heavy perfume made Janine want to turn around and leave, but curiosity forced her to remain.

"You wanted to see me, Frau Karla?" she asked softly.

For a second it seemed that Karla hadn't even heard her, but then she focused on Janine, and her face took on an ugly expression. There was a strange glow to her cheeks, too, Janine noticed.

Karla slowly pulled herself up to a full sitting position, while Janine stood there waiting for her to explain.

She could hear Emma right behind her, breathing heavily the way Hans did.

Finally Janine cleared her throat and tried again. "You sent for me?"

Ignoring her, Karla looked beyond her to where Emma stood. "Bring me one of those little blue pills!" she ordered, and Emma scurried off to a cupboard across the room.

"Are you feeling ill?" Janine inquired in an effort to be polite—and also because she couldn't think of anything else to say.

Karla still didn't answer her, and Janine began to feel concerned. "Perhaps you'd feel better if you opened some windows in here and got some fresh air," she suggested.

"I didn't ask your opinion, nor am I interested in it," Karla said rudely.

Emma walked over to the chaise and extended her hand, palm upward, and Karla took the tiny pill and swallowed it with a sip from her whiskey glass. Then she resumed glaring at Janine.

Apparently taking her cue from her mistress, Emma stepped to the side of the chaise and proceeded to glare at Janine in almost precisely the same way as Karla. However, Janine noticed that there was something resembling a smirk on her face.

"Frau Karla, you sent for me," Janine began, "and I put aside my work to come here. Would you mind getting to the point?"

"Certainly," Karla replied, her voice now sounding thick and heavy. "But surely you have some idea why I sent for you?"

"No, I don't," Janine said impatiently. She was getting tired of whatever game Karla was trying to play, and the atmosphere in the room was cloying, making her long for a breath of fresh air.

"Well, let me spell it out for you. I don't like the way you've been carrying on with my husband."

Janine was stunned. "I don't know what you're—"

"Don't interrupt me!" Karla commanded, dramatically waving her long cigarette holder. "I realize that you're not entirely to blame. This sort of thing is nothing new for André. But then it's not really his fault, either. Most women can't help throwing themselves at him—no matter how unfeminine it makes them appear!"

Janine couldn't believe what she was hearing, and her cheeks were burning with indignation. However, she managed to keep her voice calm and cool as she replied, "I really don't see what this has to do with me."

"Really? I think you know exactly what I'm talking about. Did you think I wouldn't notice the way you look at him, the way your eyes light up every time he comes near you? From the minute I first laid eyes on you I knew you'd cause trouble."

"Just what I thought, too!" Emma put in.

Karla downed the last of her drink and set the glass heavily on the table. "I have no intention of putting up with your presence here any longer. André is my husband, and you're quite mistaken if you think you can make a play for him right under my nose. You will leave Weisdorf this afternoon."

So husband and wife were in agreement at least on this matter—they both wanted her to leave the castle immediately. It flashed through Janine's mind that it was entirely possible that André had put Karla up to this, and suddenly she began to tremble with rage.

"I have no intention of trying to steal your husband, nor will I allow you to accuse me of doing so! I've done nothing whatsoever that I should feel ashamed of or apologize for!"

"Come now, don't be a fool. I have eyes, you know," Karla drawled thickly. "And so does Emma."

Janine felt like she'd been hit in the face with a bucketful of ice water. She'd completely forgotten that Emma had come upon her and André in the entry hall yesterday. Perhaps she'd been spying on them...perhaps she'd seen André kissing her hand!

"I don't want to see your face around here again," Karla said abruptly. "Do I make myself clear?"

"Quite clear!" Janine snapped. "However, you're in no position to give me orders. I work for your father and I take my orders from him. Do I make *myself* clear?"

Karla's eyes glinted with fury.

"When my father learns that you've been having secret meetings with my husband in the corridors, he'll dismiss you immediately. You can be certain of that!"

"I have had no 'secret meetings' with your husband—in the corridors or anywhere else! And I'm sure your father will be quicker to accept my word than yours!" Janine cried, no longer caring what she said. She was too hurt and enraged to hold back now even if she'd wanted to.

But what followed was as much of a shock to her as it was to Karla and Emma. Janine had given it no conscious thought, hadn't planned to say anything of the sort. The words just started to pour out of her, seemingly of their own accord.

"Frau Karla, you're quite mistaken about all this," she said in a flat emotionless voice that was curiously unlike her normal tone. "In making the accusations you've just made, you have forced me to make an announcement that I hadn't planned to make quite this soon. The fact is this: your cousin has asked me to marry him, and I have decided to accept. So, you see, it's quite absurd to accuse me of making a play for your husband."

Karla's eyes widened in total disbelief. "You're lying!" she fumed. "Frederick's a rich, attractive man—what would he want with you, a plain, penniless American!"

Janine maintained her composure. "Regardless, Frau Karla, he has indeed asked me to be his wife, and if I were you I wouldn't take the trouble to doubt it. Of course," she added, "if you find that you just can't accept what I'm telling you, you can call him in Munich and ask him to verify it."

Janine could guess the thoughts running through Karla's mind. Marriage to Frederick would make Janine part of the family—would put her in a position equal to Karla's—and that thought was more than she could bear. Her face took on a frantic look, and Emma eyed her anxiously.

"Now you can see that your accusations and your

fears are completely unjustified," Janine said as she turned and walked toward the door.

When she reached it she turned around and added, "This has been a most interesting conversation, but I'm afraid I can't stay any longer. I have work to do."

Then, her head held high, she left the room and pulled the door closed after her.

She made it as far as the second-floor landing, where she suddenly grabbed for the banister and held on tightly. Her legs were trembling violently, threatening to give way under her.

Janine stood there for a while, until she felt strong enough to return to the library. But as she neared the library she realized that she couldn't possibly do any work now. She needed to consider the enormity of what she'd just done, and she couldn't risk the possibility of seeing the count right now. If he came into the library and saw the agitated state she was in, he'd be bound to ask her about it. And the thought of having to answer his questions filled her with panic.

THE LAKE WAS QUIET and peaceful in the afternoon sun, and the sight of the swans gliding gracefully across the water was soothing to her. She stood there on the shore for a long time, lost in thought, trying to rationalize what she'd done and to predict what the outcome might be.

Frederick would be delighted, she knew, but what about André? Would he feel hurt, perhaps even betrayed? She realized that she almost hoped so—although hurting him hadn't been any part of her motivation for what she'd done.

But exactly what had her motivation been, she asked herself.

She didn't know, and now she suddenly didn't care, either. The die was cast. There could be no turning back now, no changing her mind. She'd made an impulsive, thoughtless decision—or had she?

Why shouldn't she marry Frederick? She was all alone in the world—and he was there, loving her, wanting only to look after her and care for her for the rest of her life. And he was wealthy and attractive.

The more she thought about it, the better she felt.

Yes, she knew now for certain that she'd made the right decision. She would become Mrs. Frederick Rheinberg—and she would do her utmost to make him happy, for surely he deserved that.

She envisioned him, his smiling eyes, his curly blond hair. . . . Surely someday she'd love him the way he wanted her to. She was sure of that.

Then, unaccountably, her eyes began to fill with tears.

She allowed them to flow unchecked down her cheeks. . . until suddenly there was a noise behind her, and she whirled around.

There stood Ernst, grinning malevolently—the way he had in her nightmare!

She nodded curtly to him, then turned and began to make her way back up the path to the castle. She had no reason to fear him any longer—or anyone else, for that matter. She was Frederick's fiancée. No one would attempt to cause her any unhappiness now, nor would they try to make her leave Weisdorf.

Chapter 13

Janine entered the dining room that night fully expecting another confrontation with Karla, but this time she felt well prepared for it. As the afternoon wore on she'd begun to feel better and better about her decision, and now she was ready to deal with an opposition.

However, the occasion didn't arise. Karla didn't show up for dinner, which left her alone with the count—and the ever present Hans, hovering nearby, his asthmatic breath rattling more loudly than ever.

"I'm afraid Karla is feeling quite ill this evening," the count remarked.

"Oh?" Janine replied in a mildly interested tone. She couldn't think of anything else to say.

"Miss Aubry, this is really very awkward," the count said, "but I'm afraid I must ask your indulgence for a moment." He cleared his throat, and it was with obvious reluctance that he spoke.

"My daughter sometimes has a tendency to get a

bit carried away with her...imagination. And sometimes, too, she tends to...exaggerate. Therefore, I find myself in the uncomfortable position of having to ask you to verify something she told me this afternoon...something that concerns you personally. Do you know what I'm referring to?"

Clearly, he hoped that she did, and would therefore save him the further embarrassment of having to spell it out for her.

"Yes, sir, I do. And Karla is quite correct. I've decided to accept Frederick's proposal of marriage." She smiled sweetly as she spoke.

"Ah!"the count said, nodding thoughtfully. "Then I must certainly offer you my warmest congratulations! But—excuse me for saying this—isn't this all rather sudden? My nephew never even told me he planned to...."

"I imagine he was waiting for my answer before telling anyone," Janine said.

The count seemed to accept this explanation, for he beamed with pleasure. "I'm sure I don't have to tell you what a wonderful young man Frederick is," he said proudly. "He'll make a fine lawyer and a fine husband. But then I'm sure you know that already."

Janine smiled and nodded.

"He's much like André in some ways," the count said reflectively. "They're both a credit to me."

At the mention of André, the smile froze on Janine's face, but apparently the count didn't detect it.

"Well, as soon as he returns from Munich we'll have to have a proper celebration to welcome you into the family! By the way, have you set the date yet?"

"No, sir, not yet. As a matter of fact, I haven't even given Frederick my answer yet.... I only made up my mind this afternoon."

"Surely you're going to call him in Munich tonight and tell him the good news?" the count asked incredulously.

Janine smiled sweetly again. "Well, sir, I don't think so. I think something as...intimate as this shouldn't be relayed over the phone. That would seem so cold and impersonal. And besides, I'd like to see his expression when I give him my answer."

The count's cheeks reddened for a moment, and then he burst out laughing. "I guess it's been so many years since I felt those romantic inclinations, I've forgotten all about things like that!"

Janine laughed with him, and then he continued in a friendly warm tone, "You say you only made up your mind this afternoon?"

Janine nodded.

He looked at her quizzically for a moment, then said, "Well, I suppose I'll never really understand today's younger generation. The way things happen so quickly...but then, when two people are in love, there's no point in drawing out the obvious conclusion."

He seemed satisfied with his own explanation, and fell silent as he continued to eat his dinner.

Hans, meanwhile, seemed to be listening to every word. Janine had glanced at him from time to time, trying to read his expression; but, as usual, he was inscrutable. He merely looked grim.

They were finishing their dessert, a deliciously rich chocolate mousse, when the count suddenly remarked, "I really can't understand why Karla's so upset about your engagement to Frederick. She's managed to work herself into quite a state over it."

"Perhaps," Janine ventured in a hesitant voice, "she feels he's lowering himself...that I'm not good enough for him." She knew that this was partly true, but it was by no means Karla's only reason for being upset. "And perhaps," she went on, "it also has something to do with the fact that I haven't much money of my own and have to work for my living. Maybe she thinks I'm marrying him for financial reasons."

She looked at the count for his reaction to this.

"That's ridiculous! I haven't been around all these years without learning a great deal about human nature, Miss Aubry...or I suppose I may call you Janine now, since you're almost a member of the family. But as I was saying, I've always been a very shrewd judge of character, and for Karla to think you'd marry Frederick for his money! Well, that's too ridiculous even to think about! I can tell that you're a sensitive young woman, one with a strong sense of morals and a fine character."

Janine smiled, but inside she was wondering if indeed she warranted all this flattery. What would the count think of her strong sense of morals and fine character if he knew about the night she'd slept in André's arms?

She pushed the thought away because it filled her with a terrible sadness.

FREDERICK WAS DUE to return to the castle in a few days, and Janine found waiting for him one of the strangest and most difficult times she'd ever experienced in her life. There were moments when she was tormented by fear and anxiety about the decision she'd made; and then suddenly she'd find herself feeling elated and full of hope. It was as if her emotions were on a roller coaster. Her moods swung from despair to joy and back again, sometimes within a matter of moments.

Karla was colder and more aggressive than ever, and took every opportunity to attack Janine with harsh stinging words. Whenever her engagement to Frederick was mentioned, Karla would mutter "He must be out of his mind! What could he possibly find attractive about her?"

Janine was able, for the most part, to ignore this, so that much of the time she only half heard the crude remarks. She had much more difficulty handling the way Emma glared at her as if she were a cockroach scuttling underfoot.

Karla was obviously very disturbed, and it was clear that Emma felt it was all Janine's fault. She spent what seemed an inordinate amount of time lurking in the corridors outside the library, as if she was purposely waiting to encounter Janine. When she did, her expression was so full of hatred and malice that Janine began to feel an uneasy fear. Karla was merely rude and offensive, much too drunk and erratic to be really threatening. But Emma was as sharp as a tack, and Janine sensed that she represented a very real threat. She often chided herself for being paranoid, but no matter how much she tried to convince herself otherwise, Emma seemed positively menacing.

The count, as if aware of the difficult time Janine was having, went out of his way to be pleasant. He was warm and generous, and now that Janine was about to become a member of his family, he had dropped much of his usual formality with her. At times he even called her "dear," which further enraged Karla. Still his kindness helped Janine a great deal and went far toward making her feel welcomed into the family.

As for André—she refused to think about him at all. This was no easy task, for he often crept into her thoughts. Each time this happened she summoned all her strength and directed it inward, obliterating her aching awareness of him.

But one nagging thought remained, and try as she might, she couldn't get it out of her mind: How could André manage to maintain the respect and admiration of both the count and Frederick? How could he have fooled them so completely? It was obvious that they had absolutely no idea of what he really spent his time doing when he was away from his wife. . . .

She spent as much time as she could in the library during those few days, grateful to be able to concentrate on her work—at least during the moments when her mood shifted from anxiety to hopefulness, and when thoughts of André didn't blot out everything else. She finished sorting through the birth certificates, then did the same with the marriage licenses, and found that some of her old excitement had returned. Then she began her first read-through of what she felt could be the most intriguing part of the job—the parcels of personal letters tied up in faded blue ribbons.

By the time Frederick came striding eagerly into the library late Friday afternoon, Janine had managed to quiet much of the restlessness she felt inside her. Although her moods were still swinging erratically she was able to hide this from everyone.

"God, I've missed you!" Frederick said simply as he gently drew her out of her chair and wrapped his arms around her. "Did you miss me?"

"Of course I missed you!" she said, and meant it. When she returned his kiss, it was with much more pleasure than she'd expected.

"I've got something to tell you . . . something very special," she said softly, looking up at him.

His gray eyes lighted up at the tender expression on Janine's face.

"So soon?" he said teasingly, and crushed her tightly against his chest.

"Now wait a minute!" she protested, playfully pushing him away. "I had a speech all memorized, and I intend to give it!"

"Okay," Frederick said simply, sitting down in her chair. "Now, proceed! You've got my absolute total attention!"

"Frederick," she began in a serious tone, "I've given considerable thought to . . . ." Suddenly she laughed nervously. "Oh, I've forgotten! I had it all planned, and now it's flown right out of my head!"

Frederick rose and again wrapped his arms around her.

"You don't have to tell me, darling. I think I know," he murmured, his lips brushing against her soft auburn waves. "And I think right this minute I feel happier than any man has a right to feel."

"Frederick..." she said hesitantly; "when we... well, last week, when you asked me to marry you... do you remember what I said? About people needing time to really get to know each other completely? I still feel that way. I *do* want to marry you—I know that now—but I also know that I still need more time. I want us always to be completely honest with each other, because that's the only way a marriage can work, and I—"

"Hush, darling," he whispered, holding her even more tightly. "I know what you're trying to say. You don't have to spell it out."

"But I do," she insisted, gently pulling herself a few inches away. "I need to say this, for myself as much as for you."

"All right, then," he said, and gently but firmly pulled her back into his embrace.

"Honesty is the most important thing...so I want to be honest now, right from the start. I know that your love for me is perhaps more intense than—".

"No, Janine!" he pleaded. "Don't say any more. Please."

"But I—"

"No! If you can't believe that I already know what you're trying to say, I'll say it for you. Then it'll be out of the way and we can begin building our relationship. What you're saying is that your love for me isn't the same as mine for you. All right, I can live with that. I can wait. We'll officially announce our engagement, but that's *all*. We won't even think about setting a date for our wedding. We'll wait until your feelings are more...." He broke off, unable to find the words he wanted. "We'll know when the time is right, darling. And until then, we'll work on building the basis for the best marriage in the world."

With that his lips met hers, and she was filled with amazement. How could he be so understanding, so patient, so aware of what she felt, and so willing to consider her feelings before his own needs and desires? She felt that in the space of the last few seconds her love for him had already begun to blossom.

When he raised his head, the look on his face was so intense that Janine almost couldn't bear to look at him.

"I want you to love me as a husband, not as a brother," he said.

Janine nearly gasped. How could he know so precisely...?

As if she'd spoken her thoughts aloud, he went on, "When you love someone deeply, it isn't hard to know what they're feeling. And that's why there couldn't ever be anything but complete honesty between us. I love you too much not to know your thoughts and feelings."

"I don't understand how..." Janine murmured.

"It doesn't matter. What matters is that I love you, and I want to build a relationship as beautiful and complete as any man and woman ever shared...."

His arms tightened around her. "I think we should be realistic. Right now you feel one kind of love for me, and you think that all you need is time—that after enough time has passed, somehow your love will be transformed into the kind of love you want it to be. The love of a wife for her husband. But time isn't the only thing that's needed."

Janine was deeply confused and troubled by Frederick's words, and she didn't know what to say or how to react. This was so different from what she'd expected, yet she knew deep inside her that what he was saying was right.

Again, it was as if he'd read her thoughts.

"You don't have to say anything, Janine. And we won't talk about it anymore. I've said what I needed to say, and now we're just going to take it from here, from right now, and start trying to build us the best, happiest life in the world!"

Janine looked into his face, and as he broke into that wonderful infectious smile of his, she couldn't help but smile back at him.

"And now nothing but positive happy thoughts!" he said, and kissed her lightly on the forehead. "Come on, let's go tell Uncle Albert our news. I'm sure he'll want to be the first to congratulate us!"

Suddenly Janine's face darkened. "He already was the first. . . ."

Frederick looked at her in puzzlement. "You mean you told him before you told me?"

"Are you angry?" she asked timidly.

"No, just surprised, that's all."

"Oh, Frederick—I'm sorry! I didn't mean to spoil anything. . . . But I didn't have any choice."

"I think maybe you'd better explain that to me," he said, with obvious concern in his voice.

And out it came, the whole ugly story—so fast that Frederick had to stop her several times and ask her to repeat herself. When she had finished, tears were rolling down her cheeks, and Frederick looked furious.

"Don't worry, darling—she'll never bother you again! I'll see to that!" His expression grew even darker. "Imagine! Accusing you of making a play for André! Good God!"

He was so enraged that he couldn't continue, and Janine just stood there watching as he began to pace around the library.

When he seemed to have calmed down a little bit, she asked, "What would make her do that, Frederick? And why should she hate me?"

He stopped pacing and took her gently into his arms again.

"She's a very, very sick woman, Janine. And perhaps she deserves pity more than anything else. I don't know."

"But why, Frederick? Why does she hate me?"

"She doesn't hate you . . . she's just jealous. She's always been like that—insanely jealous of any woman that André even talks to. She imagines that he spends all his time having affairs with other women, and it drives her crazy."

"And does he have affairs?" As soon as the question was out, she regretted it.

Frederick looked at her curiously for a moment. "Why, no, I don't believe he does." He paused, as if he was thinking, then went on. "If you had asked me that three years ago, when he and Karla were first married, I'd have said that there was probably a good chance that he'd eventually start running around with other women." Again he paused. "But I very much doubt that he's done that. For one thing, his sense of duty and honor is incredibly strong. And anyway, he wouldn't have time to—he devotes all his time to his Mercedes dealerships."

How could Frederick be so naive, when he was so perceptive about everything else, Janine wondered. It occurred to her, for the first time, that perhaps she'd misjudged André.

Duty and honor, she mused. André himself had used those words that day she'd met him in the entrance hall and he'd begged her to leave Weisdorf. She remembered exactly what he'd said, "You're so young—things like duty and honor probably don't even make sense to you."

Perhaps what Frederick had just told her about André was true. But, if it was, then where did that leave her? Did it mean that the encounter in the cave had meant more to him that she'd come to believe?

She couldn't even begin to deal with any of this, so she pushed her doubts away, and took Frederick's hand smilingly.

"Come on!" she said with a forced laugh. "It must be nearly dinnertime!"

Chapter 14

Janine was the first one downstairs for breakfast the next morning. She'd slept poorly, tossing and turning all night, haunted by nightmares that she couldn't really remember. She'd awakened to a gloriously sunny morning, but her mood contrasted starkly with the weather.

As she seated herself at the table in the small cozy breakfast room, she realized that Hans was nowhere in sight. Well then, she thought, perhaps she'd take a chance on a cup of coffee.... She still hadn't had so much as a sip since that first day when Hans had poured the scalding coffee into her lap.

Just then Hilda came bustling into the room, full of smiles and good cheer.

"Good morning, Miss Aubry! I'd like to be the first of the staff to congratulate you. We all love Mr. Rheinberg, and we hope you'll be very, very happy!"

Apparently news of her engagement to Frederick had spread like wildfire throughout the castle.

"Thank you, Hilda," Janine replied, with an effort at a smile.

Hilda filled her cup with steaming black coffee, and she accepted it eagerly.

"Isn't Hans on duty this morning?" she asked casually.

"Oh, he'll be here soon, Miss. He and Emma...." She broke off with a slight giggle. "They're having a few words in the kitchen."

"Oh," Janine said, but inside, her mind was racing.

Last night Frederick had said that he would make sure that Karla didn't bother her again, and right after dinner he'd excused himself and gone off to the servants' quarters. When Janine had asked him why he was going there, he'd explained that Emma was the only person who ever had any influence on Karla. And since Karla was usually too drunk to be held responsible for her actions, Emma was the one he should speak to.

Were Hans and Emma fighting about whatever Frederick had said to her last night? Janine was dying to know, but she had no opportunity to mull it over, for at that moment Frederick came into the room.

"Good morning, darling!" he said, kissing her lightly on the lips as he sat down beside her. "Sleep well?"

"Not really," she confessed.

"Well, don't worry about it. Probably just all the excitement.... And don't worry about any more problems with Karla, either. I had a good long talk with Emma, and she promised to prevent Karla from hassling you anymore."

"Hilda just told me that Hans and Emma are in the kitchen having a fight," she commented.

"Well, I imagine they—"

"Good morning, Mr. Rheinberg! Coffee?" Hilda asked, reentering the room with Janine's bacon and scrambled eggs.

"Thanks," he said, holding out his cup.

"Will you be wanting some eggs, sir?" she asked as she filled it.

"No, thanks, I have to be off soon, Hilda."

Janine looked at him quizzically.

"A surprise—for you," he said enigmatically, with a twinkle in his eye. "I've got to drive back to Munich. But I'll be back by midafternoon."

"All the way back to Munich!" Janine cried. "Why? It's Saturday!"

"It's a surprise, and that's absolutely all I'm going to say about it!" With that he gulped down his coffee, planted a kiss on her forehead, and left.

Puzzled, Janine slowly went on eating her breakfast, while Hilda refilled her coffee cup and chattered on.

"By the way," she said as Janine was getting ready to leave the table, "do you remember when I mentioned my sister, Ursula? She used to work here at the castle, but then she got married last year and opened up a little boutique in the village. Well, miss, it occurred to me that now that you're engaged to Mr. Rheinberg, you'll want to do some shopping—gifts and stationery and things like that—and Ursula's got the most wonderful selection! I thought I'd recommend her shop to you."

Janine was only half listening.

"I'm sure you'll love Ursula," Hilda continued. "She's much older than I am, and she worked here when the countess was alive and Frau Karla and Mr. Rheinberg were children." Her blue eyes twinkled merrily. "I understand Mr. Rheinberg was quite a little hellion when he was a boy, and Ursula has lots of funny stories about him!"

Janine looked at Hilda with amazement. How the girl could prattle on about such nonsense was beyond her. Why in the world would she think that Janine wanted to hear funny stories about Frederick's childhood? But Hilda was such a sweet girl, and Janine didn't want to hurt her feelings.

"Well, perhaps I'll take a drive down to the village and do a little shopping. And I certainly wouldn't want to miss hearing about my future husband's childhood antics!" she said, hoping she sounded sincere.

At that moment Hans came into the room, his usually grim expression even grimmer.

Janine got to her feet, thanked Hilda again for recommending Ursula's shop, and went back to her room.

It really was a shame that Frederick had left, she reflected, as she sat on her bed and stared out the window. She'd been looking forward to spending the morning with him, perhaps going for a walk in the woods. She'd been cooped up indoors all week, and the thought of the crisp mountain air was enticing. But after the incident with the bear trap, she wasn't about to go for a walk by herself.

Deciding to go down to the library to see if she could pick up her work where she'd left off yesterday, she ran a comb through her hair and started down the stairs. Just as she was crossing the entrance hall she met the count, who was on his way in to breakfast.

When he asked her to join him, she explained that she'd already eaten and was on her way to the library to do some work. He absolutely refused to allow it.

"It's Saturday, Janine. Take the day off!"

"But, sir, I'd really like to get some work done. And since Frederick's gone back to Munich, I have nothing else to do."

The count's eyes twinkled when she mentioned Frederick's trip back to Munich. And as for her having nothing else to do, he insisted that surely she could find something.

"Take a walk! Take a drive! It's much too beautiful a day for you to spend in the library, my dear."

"But, sir, I—"

"No, I won't hear of it. You haven't been down to the village yet, have you?" He didn't wait for her to answer, but went on, "It's a lovely little spot. Why don't you take a drive down there, poke around a little, explore the shops.... As a matter of fact, Hilda's sister, Ursula, opened up a boutique, and I understand it's—"

"Yes, sir, she mentioned it to me."

"Well then, off you go, my dear!"

Obviously he wasn't going to allow her to do any work today. She decided that it might be fun to go off by herself for a while, drive around the village... and maybe she would stop and see Hilda's sister. It might prove interesting to talk to her.

"All right, sir, I give up! I'll take a drive down the mountain."

Just as she finished speaking, one of the mirror-covered doors opened and Emma walked into the entrance hall.

"Excellent!" the count said in response to Janine's decision. Then he turned to the housekeeper. "Emma, please have Hans bring Miss Aubry's car around to the front."

"Certainly, sir!" Emma replied, with something that was closer to a smile than anything Janine had seen before.

Janine dashed up to her room, changed into a light green skirt and matching sweater, grabbed her purse, and hurried back downstairs.

The more she thought about it, the more eager she felt to get away from the castle. A change of scenery was probably just what she needed to clear her mind and chase away the lingering traces of last night's horrible dreams.

She hurried to her waiting car, glad to be behind the wheel again. Janine had always loved driving, especially on narrow, winding mountain roads where there were few other cars.

She tossed her purse onto the passenger seat, shifted into first gear, and headed down the long steep driveway to the road.

The view was spectacular as she rounded the first bend and was greeted by a vista of craggy mountain peaks with wisps of cottony clouds clinging to them. She felt filled with a peace and serenity that she hadn't experienced since her drive through the Alps on her way to the castle.

The winding mountain road was steep and barely wide enough to allow two cars to pass side by side, and every bit of Janine's driving skill was called into play negotiating the sharp hairpin turns and blind curves.

There was no guardrail on the right, and as the road twisted this way and that, she caught glimpses of the cliff that fell away some thousands of feet to the rocky ravine at the base of the mountain.

She had stayed in first gear because the incline was so steep, but now the road had leveled out, so she shifted up to second gear, relaxing more and more, enjoying the scenery. To the left was a rock-and-dirt embankment that rose sharply but not very far, for she was still close to the top of the mountain. She could see patches of wildflowers among the dirt and rocks, and the sight pleased her.

She hadn't felt this good since she'd left Paris and driven to Weisdorf, filled with excitement about starting a new life for herself. She'd been so happy then, daydreaming all the time about the mysterious stranger....

She rounded the next bend and saw that the road started to slope more steeply again, so she shifted back to first gear, rather than have to keep her foot on the brake.

André.... A month ago she'd have given anything to find him. But now that she'd found him, she wished she hadn't. It would have been so nice to go through life with warmer memories of their meeting in the cave.... But in finding him and learning the reality of the situation, her fantasy had been destroyed, her feelings shattered.

It didn't matter now. She was engaged to Frederick, yet she still couldn't stop wondering whether that night had meant anything to André.

She'd come to believe that he was just another of those married men who try to have affairs with other women. But Frederick believed that André's sense of duty and honor would never permit him to stray from his wife.

His wife . . . Janine shuddered. If André had had affairs with other women, it certainly wouldn't be hard to understand why.

The road began to slope even more sharply now, and up ahead was a tight hairpin turn. Automatically Janine's foot moved over to the brake pedal and pushed gently.

The pedal went right to the floor with absolutely no resistance. *"Oh, my God!"* she screamed.

She had no brakes!

Her hand shot out and pulled on the emergency brake. The lever lifted right up as though it wasn't even connected to anything!

The Fiat was picking up speed now, heading downhill faster and faster, the hairpin turn looming ever closer. . . .

There was no way she could negotiate that turn at this speed, and by the time she reached it the car would be going even faster! In desperation, she pushed in the clutch to downshift. There was a sickening grind and the car began to roll faster.

Frantically, her mind racing in panic, she realized that if she tried to take the turn, she'd flip the car and go right over the side of the mountain, thousands of feet down to the ravine!

Faster, faster, the scenery speeding by now, the road snaking treacherously around that curve....

And still faster... the engine whining loud, ringing in her ears....

She had no more time. The curve was right there in front of her!

Instinctively she jerked the steering wheel to the left with all her strength, and braced herself for the impact.

As the little Fiat smashed into the rock-and-dirt embankment on the other side of the road, her head snapped forward and struck the windshield.

Then everything was black....

THE VOICES WERE LOW and sounded far away. Everything was dull gray, but slowly it seemed to grow lighter, and the voices became louder, more distinct.

"...not for a week...."

"...wouldn't have found...."

"...you're sure she'll...."

With difficulty Janine opened one eye and tried to focus.

There were people bending over her. She was lying on something soft and white.... Someone grabbed her hand, touched her cheek.

She opened the other eye. Everything was a blurry haze, grayish, with shapes only barely distinguishable.

She struggled, every fiber of her being reaching out toward full consciousness. It seemed a long, long way, and she was so tired. Her head hurt....

Sometime later there were voices again, a low murmur at first, and then words:

"...no, I don't know if...."

"...soon to tell...."

Now someone was holding her hand—someone strong, whose grasp was tight.

There seemed to be a light somewhere ahead of her, as if at the end of a long tunnel, and she willed herself toward it.

One eye fluttered open, then the other eye... again, just a blurry gray haze, and shapes that she could distinguish as people. Who were they? And where was she?

She struggled with all her might to focus, to think...God, her head felt as if it was on fire!

Her eyes wanted to close, but she wouldn't let them. She kept struggling, fighting.

"You can do it...come on...come on...."

There was a man, very close, looking into her eyes, speaking to her. He looked very worried, with his solemn gray eyes.

Someone else, close to her but not as close...an old man...sparse, white hair....

Her mind began to clear, but she hadn't enough strength to speak.

The car. The accident. Frederick. The count.

"Your name—tell me your name!" Frederick was saying to her.

She looked at him quizzically, not understanding.

"Your name!" he whispered with great urgency. Then he turned to the count. "My God, Uncle Albert—the doctor was right! She has amnesia!"

It took every ounce of strength Janine possessed, but she managed to croak, "No, I don't. Janine."

Then his arms were around her, holding her close

as he murmured something to her, but she couldn't distinguish the words now.

"How badly hurt?" she managed to ask after what seemed ages.

"You're very lucky, my dear," the count answered. "It's only a concussion, but a nasty one. The doctor thought you might have amnesia, but fortunately he was wrong."

"God—you might have been killed!" Frederick cried, holding he close.

"How long...since...." She wanted to say more, but she simply couldn't.

"Frederick found you unconscious in your car when he was driving back from Munich. That was yesterday afternoon."

"My brakes...."

"You get some sleep now, dear. Hilda's right here if you need anything. And Frederick and I will be here when you wake up again."

Her eyes drifted shut....

Chapter 15

Janine was convinced that someone had tried to kill her; that the brakes on her car had been deliberately tampered with. Further, she was convinced that it had to have been either Hans or Ernst, acting on Emma's instructions.

She wanted desperately to talk to Frederick about this, because she was terrified that another attempt would be made, but she wasn't able to. She'd been only semiconscious for the first few days after the accident, at which time Frederick had maintained an almost round-the-clock vigil at her bedside. She had brief fitful periods of lucidity, followed by long stretches of deep heavy sleep. Sometimes there were periods in which she half-slept, tossing and turning, and crying out.

By the time she felt strong enough to talk sensibly, Frederick had had to return to Munich. And while he called her at least twice a day to see how she was feeling, she didn't think she could tell him over the phone.

She lay in bed day after day after day, with nothing to do but think, and her mind gave her no peace at all.

There were moments when she began to doubt her own sanity. Had someone really tried to kill her? Hans and Emma—and Karla, too—might be strange, but surely they weren't murderers; and what had happened to her car had been simple mechanical failure of the brakes, nothing more. But no matter how hard she tried to believe these rationalizations, she knew that they were just that—rationalizations, which couldn't alleviate the terror that tore her insides apart.

The only peace she had during that convalescent period of nearly two weeks was each night when the count came to her room and sat in the chair beside her bed. He would hold her hand and talk quietly with her. Each night she was allowed one glass of sherry, and she always drank it eagerly, hoping it would help to quiet the turmoil inside her.

When the count's personal physician, Dr. Schmidt, who had come to see her every morning during this period, finally announced that she could return to the library in a few days, she was filled with relief. She desperately needed something to do to keep her mind so busy that she'd have no time to feel the anxiety.

The night before her first day back at work in the library Frederick returned from Munich. She hadn't seen him since he'd left a week and a half ago, and she could no longer contain her awful suspicions. She had to tell him—to hear him say that she was, after all, only being paranoid. Then and only then she felt could she finally lay her fears to rest and go back to work.

"I'm so glad you're back! I've needed to talk to you so badly, Frederick."

"But, Janine, I told you when I left that I had a lot of work to do and couldn't get back here for a while."

She thought he seemed a bit distant, a little less loving, but she didn't stop to analyze it. Her anxiety overshadowed everything.

"Please, sit down," she said, and Frederick pulled the chair closer to her bed.

"The doctor says I can return to work tomorrow. I've felt safe here in my room, in bed, but now I'm afraid. Afraid of encountering Emma, or Karla, or Hans—and I know that I can't avoid them forever."

"Why should you feel afraid?" Frederick asked slowly, his gray eyes looking intensely into hers.

"Someone tried to kill me. Someone tampered with the brakes in my car. I've tried to tell myself that I'm imagining things, that with nothing to do but lie here thinking for almost two weeks, my imagination is working double time. But I feel so *certain*.... It's driving me crazy."

He said nothing for a few moments, and for the first time since she'd known him, she found that she couldn't read his expression.

Finally he said, "What do you want me to tell you, Janine?"

"Tell me that I'm being ridiculous. That I'm wrong. That there's nothing for me to be afraid of."

He shook his head, then said slowly, "I've thought about this a great deal. I've tried to find a way to tell you, Janine. I guess the only way is to just come out with it." He paused before continuing, "I think you may be right. I don't know for sure. But three years ago something happened that makes me think it's possible that if Karla wants you dead, she'd manage to arrange it.

"She wouldn't be stupid enough to try to do it herself, but she's quite capable of manipulating circumstances, and people, to get whatever she wants...even as far as arranging someone's death and making it look accidental."

Janine began to tremble violently. "Why didn't you tell me this last week? Why didn't you try to warn me?" she asked incredulously.

"I didn't even think about it till after your accident. And then I knew that even if I was right there wouldn't be any further trouble while you were staying here in bed, with the doctor coming in to see you every morning. And besides, I knew you needed all your strength to recover from the concussion, and I didn't want to give you more to worry about."

"And now that I've recovered what am I supposed to do? How can I go back downstairs and take the chance that they won't try again?" She started to cry, gently at first, then convulsively.

"I think it's unlikely. If we're correct in our suspicions, Emma's the one who's behind the whole thing. She's too smart to try anything inside the castle—too many people around. But just to be on the safe side, I want you to promise me you won't leave the castle at all. And no wandering around the corridors by yourself. Just stay in the library when you're not in your room."

"I'm so frightened!" she said, tears streaming down her cheeks. "Couldn't you stay here until I finish my work? Then we could go away together...."

He reached over and took her hand, then turned his face away from her for a moment.

"I told you, Janine, I have to get back to Munich. I can't give up my job right now. But I've spoken with André, and he's going to meet me here next weekend. After I've had a chance to talk it over with him, we can make some decisions."

"You said that something happened three years ago that makes you think it's possible that Karla would try to...arrange things," she said hesitantly. "Will you tell me what it was?"

He seemed to debate something within himself before he answered.

"All right. I'll tell you, because I think maybe you *should* know, so that you'll understand exactly what you're up against when you're dealing with my cousin." His voice was more severe than Janine had ever heard before.

"Karla married André three years ago, right after André's younger brother, Jacques, was killed. I know you know that much. What you don't know is that Karla and Jacques had been running around together for a year—one year-long binge in which they traveled around Europe, drunk and drugged. Jacques was a great kid.... He idolized her...he was willing to do anything she wanted, so long as she let him stay with her. She dragged him down into the depraved life that she'd chosen for herself."

Overcome with emotion, Frederick broke off. Then when he had regained some of his composure he continued. "The night Jacques was killed, Karla was with him. Not in the car—I mean with him in Switzerland. They were staying at an inn in the Alps.

The night of the accident, Jacques was blind drunk, but nevertheless he got into that car and tried to drive down a twisting mountain road that was covered with ice."

Janine shuddered at the words "twisting mountain road," but she said nothing.

"Of course there's no way to prove anything, but both André and I believe that somehow Karla manipulated him into taking the car out that night. That she knew he was too drunk to drive and she sent him out with the intention that he have an accident."

"Do you really believe that?" Janine asked, trying hard to comprehend what he was telling her.

"Yes. You have to understand that Jacques would have done anything for Karla—*anything*, because he adored her so."

"So much that he would take a chance on getting killed?" Janine asked.

"I think if Karla asked him to do something, he would do it, no matter what the danger. But you see, by the time this happened, Jacques had become as hopeless a drunk as Karla. He was probably too drunk to know just how drunk he really was."

It took Janine quite some time to assimilate this information. Finally she said, "What I don't understand is *why*. Why would she do that to someone she loved?"

Frederick shook his head sadly. "I never said she loved him, Janine."

"Then why was she spending so much time with him?" Janine asked, confused. "And how did she end up marrying André?"

Frederick looked at her in a strange manner, and

his eyes seemed to hold great sorrow. "I guess I knew you'd ask that. And I promised myself that if you did I would tell you.

"Karla had always been in love with André—obsessed with him—but he never cared for her at all. He found her drunkenness abhorrent, and her behavior disgusted him. But when Jacques was killed, Karla was two months' pregnant with his child."

"But—"

"No, Janine, let me finish. If you have any questions, ask me when I've told you the whole story. But I think you'll understand. . . .

"As I said, Karla had always loved André, and she was determined to marry him. And she never had any doubt that her being pregnant and unmarried would absolutely destroy her father. Nor did she doubt that André would do anything in his power to protect the count from such grief. Her scheme was to make André marry her—to give the baby a name, and to save the count from what we all knew would literally kill him. He'd had a heart attack not long before all this happened.

"André was enraged. She had trapped him utterly! Knowing how much he loved the count, she knew he'd have to marry her. And he did."

"But what happened to the baby?"

"Karla had a miscarriage in her sixth month—which was a blessing. I know that's an awful thing to say, but I feel it *was* a blessing."

"But if André didn't love her, why did he stay with her after the miscarriage?" Janine asked.

"Because duty and honor are the most important things in the world to him. In the marriage vows are the words 'till death do us part,' and no matter how much André had been manipulated, he did make that vow."

"But after the way she tricked him, surely he would have been willing to divorce her?"

"No, Janine. That's not André's way. He's a man of his word. Once he's given it, or made a promise, he wouldn't be able to live with himself if he didn't honor it. And besides, you know how Uncle Albert feels about family honor. A divorce in the family would be more than he could take. André promised Uncle Albert he would always take care of Karla, and he can't break that promise."

Janine shook her head sadly, filled with more remorse than she could possibly express. "So André is spending his life trapped in marriage to a woman he doesn't love," she murmured, unaware that tears were rolling down her cheeks.

Frederick looked away from her for a moment, and when he turned back to her, his expression was tight.

"It's not a matter of not loving her, Janine. He hates her! And that's part of what makes her so crazy. She thought that once she and André were married, she would have what she'd always wanted. But in agreeing to marry her he never said he would, or could, love her. In fact he swore never even to touch her. . . ."

Then, his tone suddenly businesslike, Frederick said, "I've told you what I came to tell you. I've said more than I ever wanted to say."

He rose from his chair, and Janine looked up at him in astonishment.

"I have to get back to Munich now," he said dully.

"Tonight?... Tonight!" Janine cried. "You only got here a few hours ago, and I—"

"I have work to do, Janine. And you'll be safe enough here. Just stay in the library when you're not in your room. Stay calm. André'll be here in a week, and I'll call you every night until then."

Janine was filled with fear and confusion.

She couldn't even begin to think about the implications of what she'd just learned about André's marriage. Even more suddenly pressing was Frederick's cold, aloof attitude, which hurt and puzzled her. Now there was no one to protect her from what she knew was a very real danger. Certainly she couldn't turn to the count. He'd never believe that anyone was trying to kill her, and, what was more, he would think she was crazy!

Impulsively she reached out and grabbed Frederick's hand as he stood beside her bed.

"I don't understand what's happening!" she cried.

Frederick looked down at her, at her blue eyes filled with tears, her wavy auburn hair spread out against the stark whiteness of the pillows, and he felt filled with tenderness. Tears began to mist his eyes.

"I have to go, Janine," he said softly, and pulled his hand away from her. "I'll call you first thing in the morning. But please don't worry...you'll be all right until André gets here. I'll be back soon after that."

He turned to go.

"Frederick!" Janine pleaded. "I...."

As he turned back to face her and she saw the expression in his eyes, her voice faltered and died. He looked like he'd aged ten years in the past few hours; he looked old, and tired, and desperately unhappy.

Chapter 16

Without her work to keep her occupied now, Janine knew she would go mad. She delved into it feverishly, trying to forget, at least for a little while, the pain and fear that continued to haunt her.

What Frederick had told her had made her realize many things—not the least of which was that she loved André deeply and always would, regardless of what that night in the cave had meant to him. She knew that even if it had been as wonderful for him as it had been for her, a sense of honor prevented him from allowing her to become involved in his life. She understood that now, and she respected and loved him all the more.

Her heart ached for him—for his pain, for the prison in which he was trapped—and for the love she would never be able to share with him.

Her heart ached for Frederick, too—she would never be able to love him in the way he wanted her to. It was impossible for her to feel that kind of love for more than one man. Her heart and soul belonged to André. To give Frederick anything less would be the worst possible kind of deceit, and she knew she could no longer consider marrying him. He would be deeply hurt, but she had to tell him the truth.

And then she would go away, leaving Frederick to try to recover from the wound she had to inflict; leaving André to his marriage with a woman he hated. She would leave Weisdorf and go somewhere, it didn't matter where.

All that mattered was that she leave Weisdorf and start again to build a life for herself . . . a life that she would spend trying to forget all the pain inside her and all the pain she had caused.

She knew, too, that when André arrived at the end of the week she would tell him how she felt, and how sorry she was for all the accusations she'd made. . . .

Until then she would concentrate on her work, spend every second of her time at it, so that by next week when both André and Frederick returned to the castle, her job would be finished. Once she'd told them what she had to, she could simply leave.

She had no encounters with anyone because she kept to herself. Hilda brought Janine's meals into the library on a tray, and the only time she saw the count was when he came to the library. She didn't once set foot in the dining room or the salon, nor did she linger anywhere in the corridors.

Fortunately the personal letters proved as fascinating as she'd anticipated, so that for hours at a time she was able to lose herself in them and shut out all the grief that hammered away inside her.

After studying the old marriage licenses and birth

certificates, she felt certain that there was indeed some link between the count's family and Ludwig II.

She began untying the faded blue ribbons that bound the parcels of letters, immediately struck by the crest engraved at the heads of many of them—a crest bearing an eagle and a crown; a crest of royalty.

For three days she pored over the letters; handling each parcel carefully, for the stationery was so old that it tore at the lightest touch. By the fourth day there was only one parcel left. She'd saved it for last as if it were some rare delicacy that she wanted to savor. This parcel, she knew, contained the love letters.

Knowing that the count's late wife, Hermina von Lansfeld, had been the daughter of Godeliva and Ludwig von Lansfeld, Janine had begun to form a theory. She began to read the love letters, realizing excitedly that her theory was going to prove accurate.

All the letters were addressed to "My Dearest Lola." The handwriting was erratic and almost impossible to decipher, but Janine was determined, and she spent hours over each sentence, making sure she didn't miss a single word.

In one of the letters the writer rejoiced at the birth of his son, Ludwig, named after himself. The child's surname was von Lansfeld—his mother's name. The father promised a sum of money to be set aside for this son's education. At the bottom of the letter was the same name that appeared on all of them: Ludwig Rex.

Janine knew that Ludwig Rex was Ludwig I of Bavaria, and that the woman he addressed as "My

Dearest Lola" was Lola Montez, a famous dancer and adventuress of that era. It had never been determined whether she was actually of Spanish origin because she had been born in Ireland and was a British subject, but it seemed likely. An exotic dark-haired beauty, Lola Montez had captured the heart of the aging monarch Ludwig I. It had been his total infatuation with her that eventually led to his being forced to abdicate. But while he was still on the throne he had conferred upon her the title of Countess von Lansfeld.

When Ludwig I was forced to abdicate, his legitimate son, Maximilian, inherited the throne—so that now the bastard son, Ludwig von Lansfeld, was the half-brother of the new king.

Maximilian in turn fathered two sons: Ludwig II, whose mental state was, at best, unstable, and Otho, who eventually went mad.

Having seen the official records of the count's marriage to Hermina von Lansfeld, Janine drew the obvious conclusion. Both Karla and her mother were descended from Lola Montez and Ludwig I. This would make Karla second cousin to Ludwig II, the famous "mad" king, builder of dreams and fairy-tale castles.

Insanity, or at least a tendency toward it, seemed to run strongly through this family . . . and now Janine thought she could better understand Karla's strange, erratic behavior and the wild gleam that was sometimes evident in her eyes. Of course, Karla drank excessively, but Janine realized that alcohol probably wasn't the only factor that caused her to be that way.

In discovering this love affair that dated back a century and a half, Janine had established the link between the Bavarian monarchy and the von Erlichs. Until now, it had remained hidden away in these letters, unknown to historians. Janine felt a certain exhilaration in having been the one to unearth the long-dead past.

But how would the count react to learning that his beloved wife, the mother of his only child, was descended from the bastard son of an adventuress and a king in his dotage who already had a wife and eight children?

She dreaded having to be the one to give him news that surely would horrify him, but she had no alternative.

The count came into the library in the late afternoon, as he did every day, and sipped a glass of whiskey while Janine had her glass of sherry. Each day he'd asked her how the work was coming along, and all week, as her theory had begun to take form, she'd answered him as vaguely as possible, not wanting to say anything until she was absolutely certain of the facts.

Today, however, her answers were anything but vague.

"I've found it, sir," she said, taking a sip of sherry to fortify herself.

The count's bushy white eyebrows shot upward. "You have? Why that's marvelous! Please, tell me everything you've learned."

"It's a very...romantic story, sir," she began awkwardly. "And quite intimate."

The count saw that she was blushing, and his pale

blue eyes twinkled with merriment. "Is it as scandalous as all that?" he teased.

"I'd prefer it if you'd read this letter yourself," she said, handing him the yellowed sheet of crested stationery that told of the bastard son, Ludwig von Lansfeld.

The count glanced at it, and as he caught sight of the name, he murmured, "My wife was a von Lansfeld!"

"Yes, sir," Janine said uncomfortably. "But please, read the whole letter."

When he was finished, he handed it back to her with an expression of infinite sadness, and Janine knew it hadn't taken him more than a few seconds to come to the same conclusion she'd come to herself.

"I feel...rather embarrassed, sir," Janine said softly. "It's a very private, family matter, and...."

"You're part of the family now, Janine, and there's no need for you to be embarrassed. After all, you're soon to be Frederick's wife."

She smiled as best she could, trying to hide the tears that filled her eyes and threatened to spill over. How could she tell him that she'd never be Frederick's wife, or anyone else's...that she could never love any man except André?

"I must confess, my dear, that I've suspected something like this for a long, long time," the count said. "You see, my wife was...very unstable, and toward the end of her life she became...even more so... until she finally committed suicide. She always knew that her mind wasn't... Well, you understand what I'm trying to say. And she realized when Karla was very young that...that her own daughter had been inflicted with the same sort of mental disorder. I think that was actually the reason for her suicide— she couldn't bear the knowledge that she'd passed it on to her child."

"Please, sir, don't talk about it if it causes you such pain," Janine said gently.

"Maybe now you understand why I'm so indulgent toward Karla," the old man went on. Janine saw that there were tears forming in his eyes, and her heart went out to him.

"Karla was so young when her mother . . . ." His voice trailed off, then he resumed. "It was Emma who raised her from that time on. Emma had also taken care of the countess during those last difficult years, and they were very close. So perhaps you also understand now why Emma is so protective of Karla, and why she'll do anything in her power for Karla."

Janine did indeed understand. And it didn't help to lessen her fears. . . .

The count grew silent for what seemed a long time, then finally he rose slowly from his chair.

"Janine, I hope you accept that this must never be discussed with anyone, especially Karla. She must never know!"

"Of course, sir," Janine replied. "This information will never go any farther than this room."

"I appreciate that, dear," he said, and shuffled wearily out of the library.

JANINE HAD HER DINNER on a tray in the library, as she'd done each night that week. Afterward, she tidied up all the papers and journals that had occupied her since her arrival at Weisdorf, fighting with inexpressible sadness.

Tomorrow André would be back, and she would tell him. . . .

The day after that, Frederick would be back, and she would tell him. . . .

After that there was nothing. Just blank days stretching ahead of her.

She was bone weary, and as she climbed the stairs to her room she felt like an old woman.

Tonight she would pack all her things, so that when the time came, she could simply disappear from the lives of these people and try to piece together yet another new life for herself.

She dragged her suitcases out of the huge mahogany closet, then filled them with her clothes, which were all she owned in the world; leaving only a few cosmetics out on the marble slab in the bathroom, and stowing the rest in her toilette case. . . . She went through the motions like a robot, trying hard not to think, not to feel.

When she finally climbed into bed, knowing that the nightmares were there lurking among the cobwebs that seemed to envelop her mind, she suddenly thought of the picture of André standing by the lake, with the swans gliding by in the background. Hot stinging tears filled her eyes and coursed down her cheeks.

She cried far into the night.

Chapter 17

"Good morning, Miss Aubry," Hilda said in a bright, puzzled tone as Janine came slowly down the wide stone staircase. "I took your breakfast into the library about an hour ago, but you weren't there."

"I had some things to do upstairs, Hilda," Janine answered in a dull, flat voice.

Hilda looked at her in consternation, taking in the dark, puffy circles under Janine's eyes.

"Aren't you feeling well, miss? Usually you're downstairs at the crack of dawn...."

"Everything's fine, Hilda. I'm just a little tired," she assured her in that same flat voice.

"Would you like me to bring you some coffee and something to eat?" Hilda's voice conveyed her concern.

"No, thank you.... But I would like you to do me a favor, Hilda. Mr. Gerard will be coming in sometime today, and when he does, I'd like you to ask him to come see me in the library immediately."

"Yes, Miss Aubry. Certainly."

Hilda knew better than to question Janine's request, but it certainly struck her as strange that Miss Aubry should ask for Frau Karla's husband to come to her in the library the minute he came in. . . .

Janine proceeded on to the library, her footsteps echoing hollowly on the cold stone floor of the corridor.

She had no way of knowing that while she was speaking with Hilda in the entrance hall, Emma was secretly listening to every word.

Janine sat at the long table in the library, waiting for the door to open. It was only two hours, but it seemed like a century.

How many times had she tried to plan exactly what she would say to him? Probably a hundred. And now here he was, standing in front of her, and she couldn't find any words at all.

She looked up at him, wanting to share the awful knowledge that she'd misjudged him completely, and the pain of knowing that she'd never again feel the touch of his lips or the strength of his embrace.

Whatever expression was on her face at that moment, she had no idea, but she thought it was probably a look of horror, because that's what she felt inside.

And André, thinking that she was about to start hurling accusations at him again, instinctively stepped back from the table, and slowly put his hand into the pocket of his suit jacket.

"Don't do it, Janine," he said. "Don't say anything we'll both regret."

Janine's look changed to one of astonishment as he

brought his hand out of his pocket, holding a thick letter-size envelope with her name handwritten across it.

"Before you say anything at all, read this."

He held the envelope out to her, and she took it from him reluctantly, still feeling frustrated.

"André, I have so much to say to you—about how I've—"

"No, Janine! Read the letter first. We'll talk after you've read it and had a chance to think about it."

She glanced at the envelope, which now lay before her on the table. The handwriting on the envelope was Frederick's.

She shifted her eyes back up to André, but he had already turned from the table and was walking toward the door.

"André!" she cried, suddenly feeling afraid. "Wait for—"

He stopped and turned back to face her. "I'll be waiting for you outside, in the rose garden. I imagine that letter is of a very personal nature, and I want to give you privacy while you read it, and as much time as you need to think about it."

With that he left the library, closing the heavy wooden door behind him.

Curious, she opened the envelope and pulled out three closely written sheets.

Dear Janine,
This is probably the most difficult thing I'll ever have to do in my life, but I know I must. And I'm writing it because, quite frankly, I'm a

coward. It would hurt too much to say it in person.

I can't marry you. There's nothing in the world more important to me than your happiness, and I know now you won't find it with me, as my wife.

You see, my darling, when you said you were going to try to change the love you felt for me into the kind of love you wanted to feel, you were setting yourself an impossible task. I think I knew that all along.

What I didn't know was that you already felt that kind of love for someone else. If I had known...well, it wouldn't have stopped me from loving you or from trying to make you love me, but I probably would have been a little more realistic.

As you're reading this you're wondering how I know.

That day when I pulled you out of your car, Janine, you kept muttering something...a name, I thought. I didn't really pay much attention, because all I could think of was getting you back to the castle and getting a doctor. But then during the first few days of your recovery, when you were semiconscious, I stayed by your bedside all the time. And the name you kept muttering was "André."

I know the pain you must be feeling now, loving André as you do, yet not being able to complete that love.... It's the same pain I feel myself at not being able to complete my love for you.

Janine paused to wipe away the tears that threatened to blur her vision entirely, then forced herself to continue reading.

I want you to promise me that you'll never feel so much as a moment's guilt on my behalf, Janine. You never lied to me, never did anything to try to mislead me. You were never anything but completely honest with me—and perhaps that's one of the reasons why I love you as I do.

When I heard you calling for André, I phoned him in Paris immediately and told him everything—about our engagement, the accident, the concussion. He was worried beyond belief, and he had me call him every day to report how you were coming along. I don't think you could possibly have any idea how he felt. But I knew, and it was during those phone conversations with him that I came to realize what I know now. And it was during those phone calls that I decided it would be wrong for us to marry.

That day when I found you unconscious in your car—do you remember I'd said I was going back to Munich to get a surprise for you? It was a ring. But later, when you were calling for André, and then he told me...well, I decided to return it.

I could go on and on writing to you, telling you how I feel, but I have other important things to tell you.

André and I spent a great deal of time talking last night. When I sat down to write this letter, he left, promising to pick it up this morning. By now, as you're reading this, certain things will already have been set into motion.

You cannot stay at the castle any longer, my darling. André and I agree that's it's much too dangerous for you. Therefore, André is going to take you away tomorrow morning.

Janine was stunned. Frederick was seriously concerned for her welfare. Her eyes skipped to his next words, hardly believing the urgency of his message.

I want you to pack all your things and give them to him; he'll manage to get them into his car without anyone seeing.

Say nothing to anyone. Continue on about your business as though nothing has happened.

By the time you read this, I will already have spoken with Uncle Albert, telling him that I've got tickets to the opera tomorrow night and that I've asked André to drive you in to Munich to meet me for the evening. After you're gone, I'll tell Uncle Albert the truth, explain it all to him. But don't let on to him tonight that when you leave tomorrow, you're leaving for good.

You and I both have to do something very painful right now—go on with our lives, knowing that we cannot be with the ones we love. How mixed up this is! And how painful love can become....

You probably don't yet know what you want to do or where you'll want to go after tomorrow morning. André will bring you to my house in

Munich if that's what you want. You'll have
time to think, to plan your next move. Please
don't feel awkward about this, Janine. You
needn't feel that you can't stay with me because
we've broken our engagement. I love you, and if
you want or need anything, you have only to
ask.

But if I'm wrong—if you've already come to
the same conclusions I've come to, and have
made your own plans for leaving—then André
will drive you to the airport or wherever you
want to go.

I know that André is waiting for you now, so I
won't keep you any longer. But, my darling,
please know that there is nothing in the world
more painful to him than that you should think
he was merely playing you along that night. . . .
If it meant the world to you, it meant the uni-
verse to him.

Frederick

Janine didn't need to sit and ponder the letter or the
message written between the lines. It was simple:
André had told Frederick everything; that's why
Frederick had seemed so cold and distant when he
finally came back from Munich after she'd recovered.
He'd been distant because to be otherwise, when he
knew she loved André, would have been impossible
for him. And when he'd told her about Karla and André's marriage, he knew all along about the night in
the cave.

How could Frederick love her so much that he was
willing to go through incredible pain just to set her

mind at rest—to let her know that the man she loved might indeed love her but was so trapped that he could never express it.

But there was no "might" about it. If she hadn't known that for herself instinctively, just by the way André looked at her, surely Frederick's letter had told her.

She ran out of the library and down the long stone corridor. She had to get to the rose garden where André was waiting for her. She ran so fast she didn't even notice Ernst walking along the edge of the woods that bordered the garden.

IT WOULDN'T HAVE MATTERED to her anyway. Even the pain didn't matter now. All that mattered was that she was in André's arms again, and even though they both knew that after tomorrow they would never even see each other again, still there was enormous joy being together right now. But it was a bittersweet joy, and it left them so choked with emotion that it was difficult to speak.

"I feel..." Janine murmured, knowing that there was no word to express how she felt.

"I know," André whispered deeply, holding her close against him, his lips lingering along the edge of her ear. "I feel the same."

"And after...."

"No, Janine! We won't speak of it! There's no use fighting it. Let's just stay here a few minutes longer and feel the closeness that we can never feel again...."

"I love you so much..." she whispered.

"I know Frederick told you about my marriage,

darling, but you've never heard me say this, because I've never said it to any woman. I love you. I've loved you from the moment I first saw you, and I will never love another woman." His voice was choked in his throat, as if the words had to be torn from him.

"But now. . ." he faltered. "Now we have to go back into the castle and act like everything's wonderful. I have to go upstairs to see Karla, and pretend that I just arrived a moment ago. And you have to go get packed and ready to leave first thing tomorrow morning."

"André!" Janine whispered, and rose up on tiptoe to place her lips gently on his.

They kissed again, at first softly, lovingly, then with growing intensity, until they had to pull apart. The pain of knowing that this must be their last kiss was too great for either of them to bear.

"Now go back to the libary," André said, his voice hoarse. "Tonight at dinner, while I act the model husband, you must go on with the charade that you're still engaged to Frederick."

He broke off, and as Janine turned to leave, he reached for her yet again, and pulled her tightly against him.

Finally he released her, and she ran from him, the tears hot and stinging in her eyes, blurring her vision. She ran and ran—all the way back to the library, where she threw herself down in the chair at her worktable. She laid her head down on her arms and cried and cried, until there were no more tears left inside.

Chapter 18

She'd known it would be the hardest thing she'd ever have to do, but she'd prepared herself for it. Yet seeing André and Karla walk into the dining room, Karla clinging possessively to André's arm, Janine felt such a rush of emotion that she could barely catch her breath.

Struggling to smile, she managed to say, "Good evening, Frau Karla, Mr. Gerard." Her voice was barely level.

André caught her eye for only a split second; then he proceeded to escort Karla to her seat at the table.

The count was already seated at the head of the table, with Janine to his right; André and Karla sat directly opposite her, on the count's left.

"I hear you're going to the opera tomorrow night," the count remarked pleasantly. "I'm quite an opera fan myself, and I won't tell you which one Frederick's chosen for tomorrow night, but I know you'll find it enthralling!"

Janine murmured something that she hoped sounded polite.

She caught André's eye again, then forced herself to look away. Karla's diamond-covered fingers were wrapped securely around André's upper arm, and Janine couldn't bear it.

Only an hour, she tried to tell herself. Only an hour to get through, and then dinner would be over and she could escape to her room.

She wanted to run upstairs right now, hurl herself on her bed, bury her face in the pillows, and scream with all her might.

"Yes, thank you," she found herself saying in response to something the count had just said to her. She hadn't heard his question, so she was more than surprised to hear herself answering him.

Then suddenly Emma was standing behind Janine's chair, pouring wine into her glass.

Emma!

She waited until Emma withdrew to the kitchen before she turned to the count and remarked casually, "Emma's never served dinner before. Not since I've been here, anyway. Is Hans ill?"

The count nodded. "Poor man—he had an asthma attack just an hour ago, and he's resting in his room. Emma has been kind enough to offer her services, as tonight is Hilda's night off."

Janine nodded distractedly.

Karla was drinking Scotch, as usual—and heavily, as usual. André was whispering something to her about not having another drink.

The count continued to chatter on, in an effort to

draw attention away from Karla's steadily rising voice.

Now she burst out, "Didn't you know, André? Miss Aubry here has managed to snare herself a husband. Poor Frederick!"

The count intervened at this point. "Karla, that's a very unkind thing to say!"

"Well, this is André's first night back since they got engaged, you know. Someone's got to bring him up-to-date on Miss Aubry's latest coup!"

She took a gulp of her Scotch, then set the glass down and turned to André. "Quite a performance, wouldn't you say, André? Penniless American working girl snares rich handsome lawyer."

"That's enough, Karla," André said firmly.

Janine looked down at her plate. She couldn't possibly eat, although under any other circumstances the rare roast beef would have delighted her.

"And that's enough of this, too!" André said, neatly picking up her glass and the bottle of Scotch that stood beside it on the table.

"Give me that!" Karla snapped, and tried to get the glass out of his hand.

She tried to tug his hand back down to the table, but when he simply held his arm taut, she gave up and tried to pry his fingers loose from around the glass.

With a look that seemed to contain sadness, contempt, and fury all at once, André shook off Karla's clinging hand and took the bottle and the glass over to the sideboard. There were many crystal decanters standing out ready for use, but he purposely put the Scotch bottle into one of the lower cabinets instead of leaving it out on top with the other liquor.

When he returned to his seat, Karla's face was flushed with rage.

"How dare you!" she said between tight-clenched teeth.

The count was getting very flustered, not knowing what to do or say at this point. Finally he looked at André and said, "Perhaps you'd better take her upstairs." His voice was soft and gentle, but Karla whirled around in her chair.

"You mind your own business!" she snapped.

Janine couldn't bear this. She kept staring down at her plate of untouched food, wishing that she could just fold up and die.

Then Emma was back, standing behind her chair. "More wine, Miss Aubry?" she asked in a pleasanter tone than Janine had ever heard her use before.

Janine had just finished what was in her glass, and she was tempted to reply that yes, she would like some more, but then she noticed that the bottle in Emma's hand was almost empty.

"No, thank you, Emma. I don't want you to have to open another bottle."

"Oh, that's no problem, Miss Aubry," Emma said graciously. "I've already opened it."

As she spoke, she turned and walked to the sideboard, where a newly opened bottle of wine stood just near the edge.

She brought it back to the table and refilled Janine's glass. When she had returned the bottle to the corner of the sideboard, she posted herself behind Karla's chair.

Karla was now whimpering something at André, who steadfastly refused to listen. Finally she gave up, turned her head, and said to Emma, "Bring me the bottle."

"Now, now, you'll get sick if you don't put some food in your little stomach first, Karla," Emma said lovingly. "Eat a little of your roast beef, and then we'll see."

"You give me a pain, Emma. I said I want the bottle—and I want it now!"

Emma stepped back from her post behind Karla's chair and began walking toward the sideboard.

"Don't!" was all André said, and Emma froze in her tracks. Then in a deadly calm voice he said, "Karla will have nothing more to drink tonight."

The count was getting even more flustered now. In an effort to break the tension, he said, "Emma, please clear away the dinner plates. I don't think anyone feels like eating anyway."

Emma shot a worried look at Karla, then glared menacingly at Janine, and proceeded to clear the dinner plates off the table.

Janine was confused. Emma had suddenly been so polite and hospitable to her tonight—and then just as suddenly, she was glaring at her again!

Karla was muttering something to André and André was shaking his head.

Finally in exasperation he said sharply, "Karla, this is my first night back in more than two weeks, and I have to leave again in the morning. Why make it so unpleasant for me?" Then, realizing how sharply he'd spoken, he softened his tone and added, "Surely you don't want to spoil the one night we have together?"

Janine felt a stab go through her, but she managed to hold back the tears.

"Leaving in the morning!" Karla cried. "But you just got here!"

"I have urgent business to attend to...dear," he said with obvious effort. Then his eyes darted to Janine again.

Karla didn't miss it. And she looked positively evil now.

"Aren't you going to congratulate our little researcher? Aren't you going to welcome her into the family?" Her voice was heavy with sarcasm.

André, cool as ever, turned to Janine and said with the utmost courtesy, "You're right. I haven't yet offered my congratulations. Forgive me, Miss Aubry. I guess with all the little squabbles we've been having here tonight, I forgot to tell you how delighted I am that you and Frederick are to be married. I wish you every happiness."

Janine was amazed at the suave, confident way in which he managed this, for she knew that he was hurting as badly as she was right now.

When would this meal be over? She didn't think she could take it much longer. She tried to steel herself against the tears that were threatening to break through, and the effort of holding them back took all her energy.

"I want another drink!" Karla snapped suddenly, and before anyone realized what she was doing, she had leaned across the table and snatched up Janine's wineglass.

Janine had forgotten it was there, and hadn't touched it since Emma had refilled it.

André very calmly waited until Karla had a good grip on the glass and raised it to her lips. Then he simply reached over and pried it out of her hand. It required little effort on his part, for although Karla's fingers tightened till her knuckles turned white, she was no match for André's strength.

Gathering up whatever dignity she felt she possessed, Karla rose gracefully from her chair. "I think," she said slowly, "I'll go to bed now."

She was wearing a black satin evening gown with a long velvet cape over it that tied at her neck, and as she turned to leave the table, she dramatically flounced the cape behind one arm.

Janine watched in amazement. She was the only one who could see her as she left the room, for André's back was to the door, and the count could see the door only peripherally. And Janine was the only one who actually understood what happened. . . .

Karla's arm snaked out toward the sideboard just as she reached the doorway. She snatched up the bottle of wine so quickly that her movement was just a blur, then slipped it under her cape and continued out of the room. There had been no noticeable hesitation in her movement. If Janine hadn't been watching closely, she wouldn't have seen it at all.

It struck Janine as strange that Karla would take the wine rather than Scotch, which she obviously preferred, but she remembered that André had put the Scotch into one of the lower cabinets, and the crystal decanters on the sideboard were too far away for Karla to reach them without drawing attention.

"I'm sorry you had to go through that, Janine," the

count was saying. "I'm afraid Karla is...well, I apologize on her behalf."

André said nothing. Finally he placed his linen napkin on the table and got to his feet.

Janine's heart filled with pain as she saw the expression on his face. What hell it must be for him, trapped in this awful life!

"Excuse me," he said, both to Janine and to the count. "I think I'll go finish up some paperwork I brought with me."

With that, he left the dining room.

Janine chatted with the count for a few moments more, making sure to keep her expression light, then excused herself.

She simply couldn't endure it one moment longer.

NIGHTMARES HAUNTED HER SLEEP. Low distant voices, rumblings of strange echoes, people talking, someone shouting...more voices, low, definitely male rather than female, sounding grave, ominous...and then a woman screaming....

Janine twisted and turned, trying to make the voices go away. But they wouldn't.

Suddenly she realized why. She wasn't asleep... those voices were real!

She sat up in bed, straining to hear, but she couldn't make out anything. Just distant voices somewhere in the castle.

Unable to stay in bed any longer, she rose and dressed quickly. It was just dawn now, and she could tiptoe down to the library and wait there for André. He'd already taken her suitcases sometime last night, and she assumed that he'd successfully smuggled them into his car.

But what did those voices mean? She still couldn't hear them distinctly, but they sounded louder now.

What if Karla—or, maybe worse, Emma—had seen André taking her suitcases to his car? They would think she and André were running away together!

No, she screamed inside, because she couldn't stand the thought.

She made her way downstairs quietly, knowing none of the servants would be up this early. She could get to the library without encountering anyone. Hopefully, André would be ready.

But still those voices...somewhere high up in the castle.

Puzzled, she made her way along the cold stone corridors, reaching the library at last. She inched open the heavy wooden door, and slipped inside, sighing with relief.

Then she turned around.

André was sitting at the long wooden table, wearing a bathrobe, and his face looked haggard.

Instantly, Janine knew something was wrong... seriously wrong.

The dull gray light of dawn seeped through the high narrow windows, and everything looked grainy and soft, unreal.

Janine began walking slowly toward the table, not letting herself think, not letting herself really know how much terror was coursing through her.

André rose as she reached the table, and walked

around to face her. Then he placed his hands on her shoulders, and said in a strange voice, "The police woke me half an hour ago. . . . Karla is dead."

Janine looked up at him wide-eyed and speechless, unable to ask any of the thousand questions that hammered in her brain.

His hands squeezed hard on her shoulders as he went on, "It was meant for you. Poison. Emma did it. In the bottle of wine."

Janine could only stare at him in amazement. Karla . . . dead!

"I don't know how Karla got that wine. Emma didn't know. She went in to check on her, I guess. She was dead—the police said it must have happened late last night."

His fingers were digging painfully into her shoulders now, and Janine knew it was hard for him to go on speaking, but he willed himself to continue.

"Emma confessed immediately. She said her life was over, anyway, with Karla dead. The police took her away just after they woke me. A couple of police officers are upstairs still, with the coroner."

Janine couldn't speak. Nor did she want to.

So much had happened in so short a space of time, and now this. . . .

Everything inside her was numb—numb from shock, worry, fatigue, the incredible heartache of knowing she could never have André, knowing that the bottle of poisoned wine had been meant for her. . . .

André relaxed his grip on her shoulders for a moment, then squeezed hard again.

"The police want to talk to you, but I asked them

to wait a few hours, until I'd had time to tell you. . . .

"Janine, you might've been killed!" he cried suddenly, and pulled her tightly against him.

Then he forced himself to relax his hold on her, and she pulled gently away from him. She still couldn't talk. Still couldn't think.

But as André reached out again and this time quietly took her hand in his, she knew she could feel again.

She had nothing but time now. . . time to build what she'd wanted all along . . . a new life for herself. A life with André.